The Perks of Being Alive

Joshua Britton

Bird Brain
Publishing

Evansville, Indiana

The Perks of Being Alive

Some of the stories in this collection have been previously published: "Trumpet Fingerings" in *Rhodora Magazine;* "Would You Rather" in *Night Owl Narrative;* "The Things We're Given" in *The Grind;* "The Jam" in *The Fictional Café;* "From This Tree I Hang" in *Frontier Times;* "Involvement" in *YAWP;* "Table For Two" in *Alien Buddha;* and "The Milkman" in *Nymphs.*

Cover Design: Laila Schu - Regent Promotions

Bird Brain Publishing is an imprint of Bird Brain Productions.

www.birdbrainproductions.com

Britton, Joshua
        The Perks of Being Alive / by Joshua Britton
        Summary: Collection of short stories that explores the beauty and chaos of being alive, capturing the humor, vulnerability, and resilience at the heart of human existence and the timeless search for meaning and hope.

ISBN 978-1-937668-10-5
        Paperback

Printed in the United States of America

Advance Praise for The Perks of Being Alive

A Masterful Exploration of Life's Unpredictable Journey: The Perks of Being Alive by Joshua Britton

The Perks of Being Alive is a masterfully crafted collection that captures the profound, messy, and bittersweet reality of human existence. With each story, Britton dives into the heart of what it means to endure life's challenges while still finding moments of grace, humor, and introspection. This collection doesn't shy away from the raw and uncomfortable—rather, it embraces the vulnerability of human connection and the resilience required to navigate life's most trying moments.

Throughout The Perks of Being Alive, Britton explores the enduring human desire for connection, meaning, and hope. The stories remind us that being alive means feeling the full spectrum of emotions—even when they are inconvenient or unsettling. Whether depicting the fragility of dreams or the stubborn spark of passion that persists through adversity, Britton's narratives resonate with authenticity and grace.

This collection is more than just a series of stories—it's an invitation to reflect on the beauty and chaos of simply being alive. Britton's deft touch, blending wit with wisdom, leaves readers contemplating the perks of living fully, even when life feels chaotic and unforgiving. His work is a testament to the resilience of the human spirit and a celebration of the subtle, often ironic beauty found in the pursuit of meaning amidst life's unpredictability.

Highly recommended for those who appreciate short fiction that challenges, moves, and ultimately inspires. Britton's masterful balance of darkness and light, tragedy and redemption, and solitude and connection reveals a storytelling brilliance that lingers long after the final page is turned.

- The Publisher

CONTENTS

Trumpet Fingerings 1

Would You Rather 13

The Things We're Given 33

The Jam 43

From This Tree I Hang 61

Prowler 71

Sanctuary 83

Involvement 99

Table For Two 117

The Milkman 125

No Amends 147

Twenty Years of Futility 165

"You've already found the book with all the answers

to all the questions.

So take a closer look;

You're in the turn lane, and I'm the intersection."

Mike Herrera

"Can't repeat the past?…Why of course you can!"

James Gatz

TRUMPET FINGERINGS

THE ONLY THING Ethan was better at than playing poker was the trumpet, although he sucks at both now. We don't let him play poker anymore. If I hear of a game, I follow him around to make sure he stays away.

His door is unlocked and I let myself in. There are a couple of lawn chairs in the living room with an over-turned laundry basket in between for people to put their feet on. He's fallen on hard times, which I have overseen. I'm grateful that Sammy put it on me, and not some other goon, to collect the debt, although there isn't much left to take.

The toilet flushes and the sink runs, and out of the bathroom comes Ethan. He doesn't start when he sees me.

"Hey, buddy," I say. We embrace, the bag in one of my hands knocking against his lower back.

I appreciate how easy he is to find. Some guys, when they're in this kind of trouble, bolt into hiding, and you have to track them down and rough them up worse than you normally would have had they stayed put. Ethan does me a favor, though, and is always home.

I had plucked the lawn chairs from the side of the road for him after I took his couch, and we sit opposite each other. I place the bag on the overturned laundry basket, cracked in three places. Along the wall is Ethan's trumpet, a silver Bach Strad, standing vertically on a trumpet stand.

From fifth grade through high school he and I sat next to each other in band. We became great friends. He came to my birthday party every year, and I to his; my mother still asks about him. But while I stopped playing trumpet after graduation, he majored in it in college, and he got really good. I used to go hear his quartet play. They'd play nine to eleven at The Palisade, and then linger around the bar, where someone always bought Ethan a drink. A pianist-singer duo took stage after them, and Ethan and a half dozen other guys would head for the backroom to play Hold 'Em until dawn. More often than not, Ethan would come out ahead.

The summer after we graduated from high school he worked overtime to buy this trumpet in time for the start of college. It now stands next to his gig bag, designed to hold multiple trumpets, though I've already taken the others.

From my bag I pull out two foot-longs. Ethan will only eat half of his, getting another meal out of it. I'll only eat half of mine, too, and leave the remains with Ethan for a third meal.

"Well, I guess today's the day," he says, not as morosely as one might expect.

I nod, glancing over at his trumpet, which is what I've come for. He's my oldest friend, but I do all right keeping my business from getting personal.

"I've got things set up in the kitchen," he says. This perplexes me, and Ethan sees it on my face. "Nothing fancy. Come look."

He leads me into the kitchen where on the counter sits a wooden cutting board with countless shallowly engraved scrapes from past meal preparations, and a large knife next to the cutting board.

"What the hell's wrong with you?" I say. "I'm here for the trumpet, not appendages."

"I can't part with my trumpet. Take a pinky."

"No!"

I feel somewhat responsible for his mess. Our first week of college I joined a game with some other guys who'd only known each other a few days. It was so much fun that I invited Ethan the next night. Ethan knew generally what a full house was, and that three-of-a-kind beat two pair, though it took a bit to convince him that a flush was more rare, and therefore a better hand, than a straight.

This was back when poker, specifically Hold 'Em, was really taking off, when the World Series of Poker was constantly televised on ESPN, on the heels of John Malkovich's embarrassing performance in *Rounders*. We played poker seven days a week, for as little as a dollar buy-in, which wasn't chump change when you were a struggling student, or occasionally higher stakes games with five- or ten-dollar buy-ins with five- and ten-cent blinds.

Ethan was the high blind, which was the only reason he didn't fold his three and six of spades. A hand of three-six won't stick around to see the flop too often. But while everybody called, nobody raised, and when the flop went down, suddenly Ethan was a five of spades away from a straight flush. But still nobody bet. Ethan completed his straight flush on fourth street, followed by a five of clubs on the turn.

Now everybody was hootin' and hollerin' about the fives—"all right, who's got a five! Trip fives are gonna take it!" It was checked to Ethan, who couldn't risk checks all the way around yet again, so he threw in a few measly chips. "Aww, shit, dude, Ethan's got a five, watch out!"

Somebody had to have one of the remaining two fives, Ethan assumed, or even a spade to complete a flush, but his bet was followed by folds around the table, including my own ace-ten, which had seemed so promising pre-flop. So certain were we that Ethan had a five that nobody even asked to see his cards, which in any case nobody was ever obliged to do. Ethan quietly slipped his cards into the pile, not giving a clue that we had all just missed out on the first straight flush any of us had ever seen in person until he told me about it later that night in our dorm room.

"What's the matter? You never cut off a finger before?"

"I've cut off many fingers, I'll have you know!"

"But I was wondering if I could keep it. Do you have to take it with you? As proof? Or can I put it on ice and see if the hospital can sew it back on?"

"Stop talking like that."

"Seriously, Chet, you can't take my trumpet. I won't be able to handle that."

"How the hell are you going to play trumpet without any fingers?!"

"I don't need my left hand to play trumpet. Not really, anyway. Ds will be a little sharp."

"C-sharp, too, right?" I say, vaguely recalling our group lessons years ago and the intonation tendencies for certain fingerings.

"Good memory."

"Ethan, I don't think you understand, man. You can be in the clear. Your trumpet, that model, retails at a little over three grand, new. Yours is a little banged up, so you'd be lucky to get a thousand for it. But Sammy doesn't need to know that. Dude, you're golden. Clean slate. A fresh start."

We were all so green, barely able even to spot obvious tells like grinning like a jackass or going red in the face, or a chatterbox suddenly going silent and serious. Luck was almost all any of us had; the best hand would win nine times out of ten. Ethan outgrew us pretty quickly. That straight flush was a lesson, the time Ethan realized that luck is stupid, too random to rely on. At his peak, most of his big scores came on wimpy hands like a pair of sixes or ace high, bluffing his opponents into folding better hands because he'd already burned them earlier when it had seemed to matter less. It was something to see; I was the only person to whom he ever revealed his hand after someone folded.

But he always played for fun. Once he got into trouble—once he *needed* to win—he lost the ability. And that got him into even more trouble.

He slaps his left hand down on the cutting board and picks up the knife with his right. I've never gone to the bother of a cutting board before, and I'm almost amused. But when I step forward to put a stop to this nonsense, he holds up the knife and points it at me.

"You were dealt a bad hand, man," I say now, surprised by his attack position, but un-intimidated. "You just need to play it smarter."

"There's no such thing as a good hand or a bad hand," Ethan says. "I just forgot how to play. And if you don't know how to play, all you can rely on is luck. And that never works."

If anyone pretends to be okay with losing a finger, they're bluffing, not believing we'll really do it. And after we do give them the chop, suddenly they remember a secret stash beneath the floorboards or a rich uncle they can call.

Or they bolt the next day. Because they're legitimately out of options. And we have to find them. And probably kill them.

I wouldn't be able to fake offing Ethan. Sammy insists that more than one person goes on a hit. Fortunately, that trumpet can save his life.

At the end of that first semester several of us were put on academic probation. Ethan was not. He rarely missed class or an assignment, and unlike the rest of us he wasn't bothered if he missed a game. I came back the following semester but didn't last three weeks. There was no point. With Sammy's backing, I'd done a ton of business between semesters when all our old high school friends came home for Christmas and New Years, and I committed to him full-time.

But to keep us from spending frivolously and getting into the same kind of trouble Ethan is in now, Sammy keeps track of our earnings himself and hands it out only for necessities. That's why I can't just pay Ethan's debt myself. I've tried, but what little cash I was allotted at any given moment only put a small dent in his payments, delaying the inevitable by a single week. It was a waste.

A few years later, after college and grad school, Ethan got the steady Palisade gig downtown. I went to hear him regularly. I'd request *Sugar* and *Cantaloupe Island*, the only jazz tunes I could remember from our high school jazz band, and he'd humor me—"our drummer loves *The Island*," he'd say.

I started making deals there. It was nice enough that no one would start trouble in a classy place like that.

It was in The Palisade where he asked me for help. I agreed. He'd asked with humility, but confidently, taking it in stride, and when he took the stage a few minutes later, he said into the microphone, with a wink, "this is a Miles Davis tune called *Freddie Freeloader*, dedicated to my brother Chet over there."

Several weeks later, again in the same lounge, I told him it was time to collect.

"When will you be home tomorrow?" I asked. His quartet was taking a break between sets.

"I'll be home," he said, head drooping. "I'm only booked in the evening."

"You're not going to dick me around, are you? I don't want to show up only to discover you've run off to the Caymans. Don't go dodgin' me, man."

"I'll be there, Chet, I swear," he said, his voice quavering.

"Okay. I like to sleep in. Let's plan on noon. I'll bring over some sandwiches, and we'll hang out, all right? It'll be fun. What do you want on yours?"

He shrugged and looked at me like a scolded child. "Ham is good."

I dropped two twenties in the tip bucket before leaving.

"Ethan, listen to me," I say, back in the kitchen, keeping my voice calm to grab his attention better than if I was yelling. "Don't cut off your finger. It's not necessary."

I've been bringing over sandwiches for months. He hasn't had a gig since the first night I came down on him. When I left after our first sandwich, he took out his trumpet and couldn't make a sound. No air, dry lips, fat fingers. He cancelled his gig that night and hasn't played since. But he's always been here, accepting responsibility, not giving a hint that he's a flight risk.

"Please, buddy, don't be an idiot." I take a single step away from him, toward the living room. "I'm going to walk out of here with your trumpet. We'll be square, and you can live your life."

He looks at me as if he's actually hearing my words. But he's stubborn, and he shakes his head. He has the tip of the knife on the board, the heel of the blade a couple of inches in the air, as if to chop an onion, and his pinky poised beneath.

"That's not living," he says. And he slams the cutting edge down.

We both scream. He falls backwards onto the linoleum, his head against one of the floor cabinets, then slides full body onto the floor into the fetal position, clutching his left hand, moaning loudly.

"You're an idiot!" I yell.

"It's still there!" he cries. "It's still attached!"

Dangling by a tendon from the rest of his hand is his bloody pinky. I look at it the way a cowboy would look at a horse with a broken leg. Not bothering with the cutting board, I grab the knife and, with tears streaming down both of our faces, finish the job.

"Why?!" I yell at him, fighting back the tears, pinky in hand.

With his good hand he pushes himself into a seated position. I hand him a dishtowel to soak up the bleeding.

He looks at me, with a glimmer of hope in his eyes, and says, "I got a gig tonight."

WOULD YOU RATHER

MARIN SENDS A NEW PHOTO of herself, this one taken specifically for me.

"How old is your picture?" she types.

"A year, maybe more," I type back. "I actually don't look like that anymore."

"What's different?" she asks.

"Everything."

"Everything? What do you look like now?"

"Nothing."

"Nothing?"

"Nothing," I repeat. "I don't look like anything."

THE CHECKOUT LANES are quiet. Of the three open registers, Marin is at the far end. Short and thin, she's twenty years old but might not weigh eighty pounds. She sneaks a bite of a Snickers bar she keeps beside her register.

"Did you pay for that?" Jenna accuses her from the next register over.

"Yes!" Marin insists.

"I'm going to tell Mark you're stealing," Jenna says.

"The receipt is right here!" Marin shrieks, waving the receipt in the air.

Jenna snatches the receipt out of the air, crumples it, and throws it at Marin's face. "Chill out, you freak," she says. "Stop acting like the retard you are."

Marin crosses her arms across her mostly flat chest and sulks. Her shoulders hunch forward and she struggles to catch her breath but she doesn't cry. Finally a customer emerges from the grocery aisles and goes through Jenna's lane.

I move to the right side of Jenna's register. The first three transactions I've staked out today had been credit cards. This customer holds two twenties so I know Jenna will have to open the register drawer. When she does, I shoot my hand in. I go for the twenties, but my fingers are dry and I have trouble gripping them. Jenna pushes the drawer closed, slamming my fingers in the process, which hurts like hell but keeps the drawer open long enough to buy me a few more seconds. Jenna gives her customer his change and doesn't fret about what kept the drawer from closing. I leave a twenty so at first glance she won't notice the empty slot. I look around to make sure no one suspects something is amiss before I quietly walk out of the store.

***

"THAT'S THE END of my order," I say into my phone. "But listen. Please tell the delivery man to come to the side door next to the garage. I'll leave cash in an envelope for him. He doesn't need to knock, just leave my order next to the door and take the cash. I won't need change. Thank you!"

The driver goes to the wrong door. He rings the doorbell twice and I'm worried he won't figure it out. But he finally wanders in the right direction and sees my envelope at the side door. I'm close enough to hear him mutter to himself, but not close enough to understand his complaint; maybe I didn't tip him enough; I'll have to be careful about that in the future. He looks over his shoulder as he walks back to his car. For a moment he sits there watching, hoping to get a glimpse of his mysterious customer. Eventually he gives up and starts the car, its headlights blinding me for a moment. When he pulls away, I walk to the end of my driveway to make sure he's really gone and not just hiding around a corner. In daylight hours, I might worry about the neighbors across the street, or other passersby, but at night I feel safe. I pick up my pizza and wings and go inside.

MARIN DOESN'T DRIVE. When her shift ends I impulsively tail her home.

"How was work today, sweetie?" she is greeted.

"Good, Miss Tara," she responds.

"Glad to hear it, baby."

"Can I use the computer?" she asks.

"If it's available," the nurse says. "Someone was using it last I saw. Are you hoping to hear from Joey?" she teases. Marin blushes. "Too cute, sweetie. Oh, before I forget, you didn't take your meds to work. I'll bring them to you in the lounge."

I follow Marin down the hall and into the lounge where several women have congregated on sofas and easy chairs. Against one wall is a computer. Marin sits down, logs in, and slowly reads the invitation to my house. She smiles and writes back, accepting. She minimizes the screen when the nurse comes in with a plastic cup of water and a two-ounce paper cup full of pills.

I TRY TO AVOID going to any given store more than once a week, spreading out my thefts so nobody can detect a pattern. At Marin's store again, I wait an especially long time for Jenna's register drawer to open. After cleaning her out, I tuck two steaks under my shirt before leaving.

When I open the door at home, Marin stands there, baffled, wondering if I'm hiding.

"I told you I don't look like anything," I remind her.

"I know," she drawls. After a short hesitation she walks in and closes the door behind her. "Where are you exactly?"

"Here," I say, standing next to her. I put my hand on her arm, careful not to squeeze, but she flinches anyway.

"This is so weird," she says. She's trying to resist the urge to run away, I can tell, but her feet have shuffled back a few inches anyway. Still, I admire her courage and open-mindedness, and I appreciate that she hasn't yet bolted.

"It is weird," I agree. "And inconvenient. But this is my life. Here," I say, handing her a spray bottle full of water. "Spray me."

She takes the floating bottle and gawks at it, frightened, as if I'd handed her a gun.

"I'm two feet in front of you," I say.

The spray bottle is set to mist. She pulls the trigger twice. "Ha!" she gasps. She stares, mouth agape. I can't help smiling as I feel the small droplets from the mist clinging to my skin. She sprays again. A bead of water forms on my forehead and rolls down to the tip of my nose. "There you are!" she says in awe of my outline. She sprays more, a lot more, my whole body down to my feet. My clothes will absorb the moisture faster than it will evaporate off my face, but for a moment she sees me as a complete person.

I ONLY DRIVE AT NIGHT. I go as close to the speed limit as humanly possible. I don't pass anybody, and if someone is dead set on passing me, I brake at just the right moment so the passing car will zoom by. At truck stops I use the pump farthest away from the building. To go inside for a snack, I wait by the door until somebody else goes in or comes out. I usually pee outside. After a seven-hour overnight drive, I find a parking garage with an automated ticket machine. The sun will be up soon. I curl up in the backseat to sleep for a few hours.

I aim to get to the stadium as soon as the gates open. If there's a chance of rain, I stay under cover. At home, I might go outside in my backyard when it's raining, just because it looks cool, but I can't risk it in public. Eating is tricky in the stadium because there are so few places to hide. My best bet is to stick a hot dog under my shirt and eat in a bathroom stall. Or I go upstairs to a suite that's not in use, though I still have to smuggle in food. The view from the suites is great, but most of the time I try to get as close to the field as possible, find a row with a lot of empty seats, and choose one in the middle, making sure there is no one directly behind who might want to put his feet up and wallop me in the head.

I walk along the warning track, first in foul territory and then along the outfield wall, careful not to drag my feet and alter the dirt. One time I took two steps onto the grass. I was thinking about standing next to the right fielder to trip him if a ball was hit his way. But then it occurred to me that my footprints in the grass would surely be noticed on the high-definition replays of a baseball player falling on his face for no reason. That was a close one.

MARIN IS AMUSED to watch me cook.

"This is crazy!" she shrieks. "It's like in Disney when the three fairies use their magic to bake a cake!"

A flying spatula flips a burger on the stove. A slice of cheese leaps from the counter and lands perfectly on the patty. A cup of water glides through the air and settles on the table at Marin's place.

"I love it!" she says, but then turns serious. "But how do I know you're not naked?"

"I could be," I say, "and you'd have no idea."

"Are you?" she asks. "Naked?"

"No," I answer, laughing.

"Take 'em off!" she chants. "Take 'em off! Take 'em off!"

I take off my shirt and then my pants—both of which are visible the second they hit the floor—and finally my underwear. She giggles, and I'm the least insulted anyone has ever been to be laughed at while naked. I take the burgers off the stove and place them on the buns. Marin aims the spray bottle where she knows

I must be and covers my lower half in mist. And then she giggles some more.

***

"IT'S NOT AS GREAT as you would think," Justin says to me. "If I could go as fast as Superman, or even Peter Pan, it would be awesome, but when I'm up there, birds whiz by me like nobody's business. For the most part, it would be faster to walk."

Justin mows my lawn. I do the backyard, and the part of the side yard that's mostly obscured, where there's little chance of anybody seeing a lawnmower operating by itself. Justin does the rest. He feels guilty because in our game of *Would you rather...*, he got to choose his superpower first, and he chose flying.

He's just finished and we're in the backyard where the chicken on the grill is just about done. Unlike Marin, he tries to act cool, like it's normal to see food flipping itself.

"It's an incredible sensation," he continues. "I won't deny that. But I can't just float around town with everyone seeing me. It would raise too many questions. I'd be a freak show. I wouldn't get a moment's privacy"

"Yeah, I get that," I concede, not feeling the least bit sorry for him because I have the exact opposite problem—too much privacy. "But you can simply choose not to fly and go about your life as if it's perfectly normal. But me? I can't turn this off."

"I know, man, and I'm sorry," he says. "That's why I do this," he says gesturing toward the lawn. "I'm here to help."

"I can only use my powers for evil," I say. "And it sucks, to be perfectly honest."

"You went into the women's locker room, though, right?"

"Yes," I admit, begrudgingly, because we've talked about this before.

"And…?"

"It's not that great! I don't like this. I don't feel like I'm a bad person, but I'm doing bad things."

ONCE AGAIN I STAND poised next to Jenna's register. The first time she opens her drawer I take most of the fives. I'll count them later but I doubt it's more than sixty dollars' worth.

Marin tells me everything. She tells me about her family whom she's hardly seen since she turned eighteen. She tells me about the social worker who got her this job. She tells me about her struggles to get her Items Per Minute up to store average. And she tells me about the times Jenna is mean to her. Jenna throws crumpled-up receipts at her and accuses her of stealing. Jenna tells her she looks like a boy, even though she's worked hard to grow her thin scraggly hair chin-length. Jenna tells the other cashiers Marin is anorexic and retarded.

A customer pays with a hundred-dollar bill. Jenna puts the hundred underneath the till, along with any other big bills customers may have paid with. It would be unrealistic to try to lift the till quickly enough without being noticed, so I help myself to her small stack of twenties.

I stop at the bank on my way home to deposit the cash using the outdoor automated teller. I'll keep taking from Jenna's drawer until she's fired.

I PICK MARIN UP and even though she locks her arms around my neck, it freaks her out to look down and see herself floating three feet above the floor. But she grows to love it. She asks me to pick her up in front of a mirror. She weighs as much as a child, and I can't help treating her delicately. She wants to take a picture of herself on my shoulders, and I say only if she doesn't show it to anyone. She lies flat across my outstretched arms and, with her arms out as far as they can reach, she looks like she's flying, like a baby bird.

"Flying's overrated, too," I tell her.

Lying in bed, I'm compelled to remind her of the old picture of me, and to assure her that I'm not an unattractive person, that it's not like I became the way I am so as to cover up grotesque deformities. She keeps the spray bottle within an arm's reach and I'm constantly damp. Sometimes I spray her back, and she squeals with jollity. She has a long and crooked scar that runs from her waist to her hip, too long and out of place to be from appendicitis or a kidney transplant. She doesn't mind when I trace it with my finger. She has another scar on the side of her head, mostly obscured by her hair.

"I will take care of you forever," I whisper.

"I HAVE A GIRLFRIEND."

"Oh?" Justin's interest is piqued and he raises his eyebrows.

"I met her online," I say.

"Oh, that makes sense," he says, disappointed, eyebrows lowering. "The loneliness is getting to you, isn't it? I imagine it would drive me crazy, too."

"I've been pretty lonely, yes," I admit. "But I feel great now that I have Marin."

"Marin?"

"My girlfriend," I say. "I've been seeing her for over a month."

"Seeing her, huh," he says. "But has she been seeing you?" He laughs. "Sorry, buddy. I'll try to fly over more often."

***

I TRY TO FIND a legit means of making a living. I apply for several jobs which would enable me to work within the privacy of my home. An e-mail response to one of my applications contains a request for a Skype interview. If only this were twenty years earlier, before Skype was a thing. I could tell them I don't have Skype, and request a phone interview instead, but the job is dependent on having a high-functioning computer, which would certainly have video chat capabilities. So this job will not work out.

I take in a poker game at the casino. I haven't mentioned this to Justin yet, but my idea is to sneak around the table and whisper the other players' hands into Justin's ear. We'd split the winnings. I'd have to be able to run around the table easily, so it couldn't be too crowded—no Fridays or Saturdays—which would probably mean lower stakes. Still, I'm optimistic that it could work.

Another idea: jumping over the counter at the bank doesn't seem like it would be terribly difficult. At the grocery store I rarely come away with more than a hundred or two at a time, and I have to assume that soon some sort of investigation will be launched. A big score at a bank every other month in the surrounding counties and states might be the answer.

ON TV there is a tabloid-style news report of a flying man. Several people claim to have seen him, and there is cell phone footage, too, but the flyer is too far away in the video, and the resolution on the zoom-in too poor, so the flyer remains unidentified.

A hard pounding rattles the front door. I turn off the TV and look out the window.

"Two nurses from your home," I tell Marin. "Miss Tara is one. I don't know the other."

"I wonder what they want," she thinks out loud, more confused than scared. She gets up to answer the door.

"Don't," I say. "Hopefully they'll leave."

"You in there, Marin?!" one of the nurses calls out.

Marin slinks back into the couch, legs folded to her chest so that her chin rests between her knees. I put my finger to my lips, but of course she can't see, so I say, "shh." She stifles a giggle.

"We know someone's in there!" the nurse calls again. "We could hear the television!"

"This is silly," she says to me, and then she shouts, "I'm coming!"

"No!" I whisper harshly. I turn to hide before remembering I have built-in camouflage.

Marin opens the door and enthusiastically greets the nurses. "Hi, Miss Tara! Hi, Miss Rachel! This is Joey's house!"

"Joey's house, huh," Miss Rachel says with obvious skepticism. They both come in and Marin closes the door behind them. "I'd like to speak with Joey."

"Oh, sure!" Marin says. "You just can't see him. Joey, come say hello!"

Marin stares across the room, where she thinks I might be. Nobody but Marin and Justin has been in my house for such a long time. I haven't been this frightened since coming to grips with my new life. Very slowly I back away, trying hard not to make a sound as I slide on my socked feet, but a floorboard creaks anyway. At that the nurses' ears perk up, and for a brief second they believe Marin.

"Joey, where are you? Please say something," she pleads.

"Good grief, Marin," Miss Rachel says. "This is breaking and entering."

"Oh!" she says, coming up with an idea. "I know!" She grabs the spray bottle from the ottoman and sprays several times in various directions, but I'm ten feet out of range. "Joey, where'd you go?" She sprays again. "Joey, please talk to my nurses." She sprays more, but still doesn't hit me. She sprays behind her, slowly spinning, fingers pumping the water in all three hundred sixty degrees, gradually speeding up, soaking the entire living room like a sprinkler, shrieking, "Joey! Where are you?! Help me, Joey! Come back!"

"Marin, you're getting us all wet!" Miss Rachel exclaims, trying to get out of splash range, while Miss Tara encloses upon tiny Marin, enveloping her in her big arms. Marin is crying. She lets go of the water bottle and it thuds when it hits the ground.

"He was just here," she sobs. "You can't see him. He doesn't want anyone to know about him."

"Just you, right, baby?" Miss Tara says, soothingly, rocking Marin back and forth.

"Just me," Marin says through her tears.

"We need to get out of here," Miss Rachel says. "Come on, Marin. Let's get you home."

"Okay," she sniffles.

MARIN SITS ON THE EDGE of her cot with her feet dangling inches off the floor. Her hair has been cut short, not quite a buzz, but close. Jenna would make fun of it, if I hadn't gotten rid of her. Keys jiggle on the other side of her door before it opens and Miss Tara comes in.

"Hi sweetie, time for your meds," Miss Tara says.

Marin nods. The nurse gives her a two-ounce paper cup full of pills. Then she fills a cup full of tap water at Marin's kitchenette so Marin can wash the pills down.

"Open up," Miss Tara says. She shines a flashlight into Marin's open mouth. "Lift your tongue, please," she says. Marin does as she's told. "Good girl," the nurse says. "Drink the rest of the water, please."

Marin gulps it down and hands back the cup. "Thank you, Miss Tara."

"You're welcome, sweetie. How was your day?" she asks. "Have you heard from Joey?"

"I didn't see him today," Marin says. "But I never saw him anyway."

"You didn't?" Hope flashes across Miss Tara's face.

"No," Marin says. "He's invisible. He sent me a picture once, but it was a year old."

The nurse deflates, her shoulders drop. She puts her hand on Marin's cheek, and Marin leans into it.

"Hang in there, sweetie," she says. "We'll get this figured out."

The nurse leaves and again there are jiggling keys on the other side of the shut door. I pull on the handle and push, but the door is indeed locked from the outside.

"Joey?" Marin whispers, leaning forward. "Joey, is that you?" She stares intently at the door handle which she is so sure she saw move a moment ago. "Joey? Are you there?"

"I'm here," I say. I pull the water bottle out from under my shirt. She suppresses a shriek as the bottle floats her way. She sprays me with mist.

"Oh, Joey, it *is* you!" she says, springing off the bed and giving me a big hug. I bend over and we kiss.

"Oh, Joey, I'm so sorry. I should've kept quiet. I should've pretended nobody was home, like you said. I'm sorry, Joey. Joey, they said I can't work anymore. They said I can't leave the home anymore. I can't use the computer either. But that doesn't matter as long as you're here."

"I'm here," I repeat.

"It doesn't matter," she repeats. "I don't need to work or go outside. It's just so great to have you here. Will you stay here with me?"

I look around her room—no TV or computer, no bookshelf, no window, an unenclosed toilet in the corner.

"I'll stay here with you," I say.

I lie down on the bed and pull her next to me. Her scar is easier to see with her short hairdo. We kiss again and I put my hand under her shirt, on her side.

"Are you feeling my scar?" she asks.

"Mm-hmm," I say.

"I like being touched by you," she says.

It's nice not being alone. My hand on one scar, my nose on the other, we spoon on her cot until we fall asleep.

THE THINGS WE'RE GIVEN

A STRETCH IN LATE FEBRUARY had been un-seasonably warm and the water level was low. Walking upstream they came to a bend where a pile of garbage rested on a patch of dirt that would be under water later in the spring. Some of the garbage was so dirty it had likely been there for weeks, while other pieces looked fresher.

"Maybe your bottle will end up there, too," the man said, annoyed.

"I already said I'm sorry!" the boy cried.

They'd been throwing twigs into the water, watching them float lazily down the creek and passively collide with protruding rocks, gradually drifting out of sight. The man marveled at the boy's fascination with throwing things into the water. He'd done the same thing thirty years ago. Actually, he still liked to throw things. Thousands of years ago, cavemen probably threw sticks with their sons, too.

The boy had finished the Pepsi that he and the man had been taking turns drinking and threw the empty bottle into the water. The current took the bottle, something colorful to watch amidst the grays and browns of the sky, dead grass, and mud.

"Hey!" the man had scolded. "Don't be a litterbug!"

He'd rushed to the edge of the bank, grabbed a longer stick from the ground, and tried to reach the bottle. But it was out of reach. The bottle gravitated to the far bank, ricocheted softly off the edge, and sailed further and further away.

"Good job," the man had said sarcastically. "You always preach about nature, and then you do something like that. What were you thinking?"

The boy's lower lip jutted out and quivered, his eyes moist, and the man felt bad.

"Just don't do it again," he said, less harshly. He ruffled the boy's hair, out of pity.

He'd been trying to impress upon the boy the importance of taking care of the things he'd been given; one should take care of the earth, just as one should take care of his home and his body. The Pepsi withstanding, the boy ate healthily, was physically active, and was generally willing to carry a wad of garbage in his pocket for as long as it took to find a garbage can, or carry a soda can even longer to a recycling bin. None of this teaching, however, seemed to apply to picking up the toys and litter on the floor in his bedroom. The boy, who often walked back and forth in perpetual motion between the rooms of their house, would step over things on the floor rather than pick them up. The man likened the boy to an aquarium shark that never really stopped moving as it glided nonstop around its tank.

"The great white shark isn't actually the most dangerous shark," the small boy loved to instruct. "The bull shark can survive in fresh water and is more agg-ressive to humans."

"I wouldn't want to run into either one."

They'd been watching a lot of Animal Planet, and for every program that showed a great white jumping out of the air to catch a seal in its jaws, there was another that showed animals swimming in floating debris, seals covered in oil, and fish caught in six-pack rings. The boy had begun to feel disdain for the human race.

"The camera guys are going to help him, right?" the boy asked about a polar bear. With summer approaching, the polar bear's habitat was breaking off into the sea and floating away. The polar bear had waited too long. Realizing that it was past time to relocate for the season, he began swimming for a more permanent residence. But, according to the narrator, he was disoriented, and while polar bears can swim great distances, there was no land for hundreds of miles in the direction he was headed. He would drown.

"They're not supposed to interfere," the man said. "Just observe and document. Besides, polar bears are dangerous, and they could get hurt."

"Who cares about them! The polar bear is going to die!" the boy wailed.

Not long before that he'd dedicated his life to science, and at the age of six he had much of his life ahead of him. He'd resolved to be a scientist, the kind who would risk his life to save a confused polar bear.

By the end of a week of zoo camp the previous summer, he'd grown exponentially more mature.

"There's a lot I still need to learn," he told the man as he tried to make sense of the earth's axis and its relation to the seasons. "That's why I'm going to be a scientist and work in a building where all different kinds of scientists work. It's pretty big, I bet."

"I bet it is, too," the man agreed. "Where is this building of scientists?"

"I don't know," the boy said. "I think I need to ask some construction workers to build it. Maybe I'll be a construction worker first."

The zoo camp was a great success, though the boy confessed he wished they'd played fewer games so they could do science all the time. He wanted to measure a zebra's temperature with a thermometer, for instance. He wanted to feed the lion and take its pulse. He discovered he didn't care that much for birds, although he liked it when the little budgies landed on him in the interactive exhibit.

The man resolved to expose him to nature more often, and they went hiking. A groundhog crawled by as they sat in a grassy clearing eating their sandwiches. Otherwise, they didn't see much wildlife beyond horseflies, deer, and a snake so quick they couldn't tell the species. The boy brought along a notebook to record his observations—

All horseflies are monstrous horseflies, he wrote.

"I wish there weren't any people here," the boy said every time they passed another hiker. "They're probably scaring all the animals away."

"We're probably scaring them off, too," the man pointed out.

The boy stopped cold and planted his feet to the ground. He held his breath and listened intently, scanning the woods. Finally, he turned to the man and grinned wildly.

"Well now I really don't know what to do!"

They were new to this city, and the man couldn't remember seeing so much garbage along the roads any-where else he had lived. He was tired of moving and didn't want to be there in the first place, so he may have been prone to notice the negatives. But he had never found it difficult to put things where they belong: dishes in the dishwasher, coats in the closet, garbage in the garbage can. People make mistakes, he acknowledged; just the other day his grocery store receipt had slipped from his hands and blown across the parking lot. But the volume of garbage along the ramp to get onto the expressway could not have happened solely from accidents.

They walked on. The creek narrowed and there were stepping stones so close to each other that even the boy with his short legs could hop from one to the next. On the other side now, they reversed direction and came back to the accumulation of garbage they'd seen earlier. And sure enough, there was the boy's Pepsi bottle. Either they hadn't spotted it earlier, or enough time had passed for it to join the heap.

The man contemplated his own selfishness. If he were a better person, he thought, he would fetch a 32-gallon garbage bag and clean the creek up. But he didn't want to pick up other people's garbage, just as he rarely picked up garbage anywhere unless it had blown into his own yard. And with a pile like this, he could get cut by broken glass or stabbed by a disease-ridden hypodermic needle. Still...

"I think we can reach the bottle," he said. "What do you say? Want to tag team?"

The garbage wasn't floating but had collected on a slab of land only millimeters above the water level. They inched toward the water's edge. Between them and the garbage was mud with perhaps a half an inch of dirty standing water.

"Watch out for the mud," he'd pointlessly been saying all day. What little snow they'd gotten had melted, but it hadn't been warm enough for the ground to dry out. Telling the boy to watch out for mud was like telling kids cigarettes cause cancer while selling them a carton from the trunk of a parked car.

Neither he nor the hopeful boy were wearing boots. In fact, the man's athletic sneakers had ventilation netting on the sides that would freely admit unwanted moisture. He held onto a young tree, narrow in diameter, gradually shifting his weight toward the bottle, leaning over the marshy section, extending his reach. But he didn't come within a foot of the bottle.

"Come here," the man said to the boy.

He eased the boy down the side, holding him tightly, still able to reach with one hand all the way around the boy's little wrist. The boy, now an extension of the man, was able to get a fingertip on the blue bottle. The bottle had been there for only a few minutes, knocking at the side, and was not entrenched in sediment like much of the garbage. After a bit of rocking back and forth, the boy was able to finagle the bottle loose from its temporary resting place and bring it close enough to get a grip.

"I got it," he cried triumphantly, holding it by the cap end.

"Good boy!" the man congratulated. "Throw it up onto the grass."

Still hanging from the man's grip, the boy heaved the bottle in the direction from which he hung. But his off-balance toss fell short of the higher land and was about to roll back into the mud. The man batted the bottle with his hand and volleyed it clear of the creek.

But while he hadn't let go of the boy, his other hand had been gripping the tree. They both toppled toward the mud. The boy went in face first. The man had a tad more time to brace himself and landed up to his elbows in mud, thankfully shy of the refuse pile.

"Ohhh," the man moaned.

The boy looked out of science-fiction, with only the whites of his eyes and teeth to suggest a human child. And he laughed, a high-pitched giggle. The man adored his giggle; anything was worth hearing it.

"Thanks for helping me get the bottle," the small boy grinned.

The man reached out to help the boy up, but the mud was too slippery and neither of them could get a grip, so the boy stood on his own.

THE JAM

A BLACK NISSAN HATCHBACK with its lights off rolls down the street. Zane is at the wheel, and he and Brandon listen through the open windows for community unrest. But it's dark and quiet. The lights go off at 11:00, inside and out, whether you're ready or not.

Utopic villages like this one have sprouted up all over the country, segregation as a result of a rigorous application process. Zane had tried to be admitted just hard enough to know it was futile. These communities were designed to keep out gimps like Troy and minorities like Brandon. If discovered, how they'd snuck in would cause a panic among the residents.

Aided by light from the moon without the hindrance of light pollution, Zane slowly navigates the hatchback toward the main gate through the flat neighborhood landscape without having to rev the engine.

At the end of the drive, the main gate is closed. Brandon gets out to test the fence, but it's locked and he doesn't have a code. It's dark here, too, except for the faint glow of the keypad. The sturdy double-layered fence appears primed to prevent little putt-putt Nissans like theirs, chosen not for its strength but because it was cheap and black, from driving through it. Zane hobbles to the gate. How many digits could it be? Probably four or five. He picks five, and punches in 6-7-1-9-4. It doesn't work. 1-4-3-9-8. That doesn't work either. 8-7-8-0-2. Nope.

"You're guessing," a staticky voice sounds through the intercom next to the pad.

"Excuse me?" Zane says, jumping.

"Did you forget your code? Or are you simply shooting in the dark?"

"We were just visiting," Zane says. "I was given a code, but I can't remember it now. Can you let us out?"

"Where are you coming from?"

"We were at the Millers."

At that, Brandon shoots Zane a look. The Millers? Zane shrugs. Good bet that somebody in a waspy community like this is named Miller.

"All right," the voice says. "I'll be right there."

Zane and Brandon look at each other in the moonlight, wide-eyed, and together they glance upward to the top of the fence. Falling over each other, they rush for the back of the car. Zane unlocks the hatch and Brandon picks up the bag.

"Over here," Zane says, gesturing to a bushy side of the gate. Of the two, Brandon is much bigger and stronger. He heaves the bag high into the air, but just misses the top, and the bag falls back to their feet. Zane cringes to think of the damage. "Hurry!" he hisses. "Try again!" A flood light suddenly turns on and illuminates the entire area. Brandon heaves the bag harder, and this time the bag clears the fence and lands with a heavy rustle in the shrubs on the other side.

A moment later an SUV rounds the corner and pulls up behind the Nissan; Zane is mortified to realize that the hatch of the car is still open. Clayton steps out of the SUV, flashlight in hand, and peers into the open trunk. The back hadn't been open when he'd left his monitor to join them at the gate, but he doesn't spot anything.

"Your memory must be worse than my grandfather's," Clayton says, "and he's ninety-eight years old with Alzheimer's." He walks over to the two strangers; the big bald one is even larger than he had looked on the screen. "It's a six-digit code, not five. Everyone has a personal code," he goes on. "And no one should be giving theirs out. We'll talk to the Millers about that."

Brandon cracks a smile.

"I don't want to get them in trouble," Zane says quickly.

Clayton nods. "Of course you don't," he says. "Follow me. We'll get this sorted out."

"We're in a bit of a hurry," Zane says. "Stayed too late. I'm sorry for causing any trouble, but it would be really helpful if we could just be on our way."

Clayton nods some more. "This won't take long. Follow me."

He gets into the SUV and pulls ahead of the Nissan to wait for them along the side of a road parallel to the fence. The fence, Zane knows, covers the entire peri-meter of the community, and is equally effective at keeping the unwanted out as at keeping people in. The main gate and a rarely used emergency-only gate are the only ways in or out. Even if they ran for it, it would only be a matter of time before they were sniffed out.

They had gone unnoticed until arriving at the gate. Clayton wonders how they'd gotten in in the first place. The two strangers take a minute to get into the car and turn in the right direction. Driving slowly so they don't have a chance to bolt, Clayton leads the way to a vast parking lot next to a warehouse and some off-ices. The security offices are in front, closest to the housing, off to the side of the cafeteria where only a few overnight warehouse workers are taking breaks. The residents, guaranteed work and protection, would be agitated if they knew of this breech. At this hour, the coffee shop is open, but nothing else.

Brandon and a limping Zane follow the guard's lead to his office where they are seated in front of a desk. Because of the blackout mandate, the complex should be the only lit building in the community. Under the fluorescent lights Clayton takes them in, the confident façade of the little one, the darker complexion and wide eyes of the big bear who has not gone bald, he observes, but shaves his head, a habit Brandon hasn't broken since discharging from the army. He is an imposing figure, hair or no, and the other one looks harmless at his side.

"Do you guys want some coffee?" Clayton asks, his nametag now visible in the light. "I'm going to get some for myself."

"I take it black," Zane says. He looks at Brandon, who shrugs. "Two blacks," he tells Clayton.

"I'll be back momentarily," Clayton says. "Make yourselves comfortable."

Considering the ease of getting in, neither Zane nor Brandon had been overly concerned that it would be difficult getting out. And what Zane had said about being in a hurry wasn't smoke. Brandon has a flight to catch in a few hours, and before that they will need to pick up his suitcase at their hotel. The goods they threw over the fence will need to be unloaded.

"Your flight is at 6:30, right?" Zane asks with Clayton gone. "To Pensacola via Atlanta?" Brandon nods.

Once Zane's favorite conversationalist, Brandon has been mute since returning from the war. In Pensacola Brandon had been set up with a nice gig cooking at the VFW where he rarely saw anyone who hadn't dealt with similar trauma. But outside of the VFW, things had gone badly, and it was no longer safe for Brandon to live there. Nor would it be safe for several others if he wasn't able to tie up loose ends, loose ends that hinged on the contents of the bag they'd thrown over the fence. But a couple of loyal friends were going to get him onto a boat that would set sail into the gulf at midnight, fewer than twenty-four hours from now and a thousand miles away. He would leave the country forever.

"I'm not going to mention the boat to this guy," Zane says. "But we need to get you out of here. Even if I have to stick around; I don't care; no big deal. But you need to get on that flight. This guy seems nice enough, but if you're still here when people start waking up, you'll get torn to bits."

Brandon turns his head toward Zane and nods.

The community directory is on a bookshelf next to the door.

"Keep a look out, will you?" Zane says.

Brandon pokes his head out the door while Zane pores through the book. There is a Miller, but just one, a single guy, and elderly. They could say they were visiting a grandfather or a great-uncle. Zane decides against that. He flips the book some more. Wilson—Melissa and Stephen, and three kids, Danielle, Reese, and Lyle. Zane decides that Clayton heard incorrectly before. The Wilsons will work much better. In real life, Zane has a cousin named Melissa, and he prefers his lies to have some truth to them.

Brandon violently snaps his fingers. Zane quickly memorizes the first names of the Wilsons and shoves the book back onto the shelf with seconds to spare, putting pressure on his leg the wrong way, stifling a whimper.

Clayton re-enters holding three coffees in a four-count disposable carrier. "Two blacks," he says, handing two cups to his guests. "And for me," he says, taking the third, "lots of cream, lots of sugar. I ordered some sandwiches, too. She'll bring them to us." He notices Zane's face trying to conceal pain. "What's wrong with you?"

"I have a bad leg," he confides.

They all take sips. Brandon, who doesn't usually drink plain black coffee, briefly chokes. Zane whacks him on the back.

Clayton is amused to see the big one taking a hit from the little one. "The Millers, huh," he says, smiling. "How do you know them?"

"The Wilsons," Zane faux-corrects. "She's my cousin. Melissa Wilson. Her husband's name is Stephen. Steve, really. They've got three kids."

"You said Miller before."

"I don't know any Millers. Melissa's last name is Wilson."

"You sure? Could've sworn you said Miller."

Clayton's office is small for being part of such a gigantic complex. Since he hadn't wanted to share an office with the other security directors, he volunteered to take this little offshoot of a room, formerly a storage closet. During the day, thousands of workers filed through the turnstiles and mill about the complex warehouses, comings and goings meticulously tracked. At lunchtime, between 11:30 and 1:30, it is nearly impossible to find a place to sit. Fewer than one hundred employees worked overnight.

He yawns. He doesn't usually have anything to do at this hour.

"So you're sticking with Wilson. Well, let's give Melissa a call," he says, grabbing the directory from the bookshelf, noticing that the directory has been slightly misplaced in his brief absence. "Or Stephen."

"I wish you wouldn't," Zane said. "It's so late, and she and Steve went to bed before Brandon and I even left. I'd hate to wake her up and get on her bad side."

"That doesn't give us a lot of options, then," Clayton says, putting the directory back, this time correctly. "Short of sitting here together for the next few hours until the morning bell goes off."

"Well, it's not a big deal for me to wait," Zane says, confident in his ability to weasel out of this. "But my boy here's got a 6:30 flight, and they say you should get to the airport two hours ahead of time. Plus, he's got to get his suitcase from our hotel, so that's another two hours to get from here to the hotel to the airport. It's after one now, so he really needs to hit the road soon."

"Where you going?" Clayton asks Brandon.

"Pensacola," Zane answers.

"The panhandle! What are you going to Pensacola for?"

"He lives there."

"Does he always speak for you?" Clayton asks, intently directing his question at Brandon.

Brandon doesn't say anything, and after a few seconds he glances at Zane for help.

"Not exactly the loquacious type, huh," Clayton says.

"He doesn't talk since Iraq," Zane explains.

"Oh," Clayton says, sympathetically. "I'm sorry to hear that. Thank you for your service."

"He cooks at the VFW down in Pensacola."

"Very good," Clayton says. "Well, I can probably get you a ride to your hotel, and then to the airport—" Clayton stops abruptly and sits up straight. His intestines churn and gurgle loudly enough to be heard on the other side of the desk. "Excuse me," Clayton says, carefully rising from his chair and waddling out of the office, clenching his rear end as he goes.

Brandon looks at Zane, accusing him of tampering with the guard's coffee.

"I didn't do anything," Zane says. "When could I have possibly done anything? But listen, if he sets you up a ride, don't forgot to find a way to pick up the bag in the bushes. Knock out the driver if you have to. All our heartache will go to waste if we don't come out of here with that bag. I can deal with whatever as long as you get away."

Always the biggest kid in school, Brandon was an outcast like Zane, but he was rarely picked on. He could knock out anybody; it was always only a matter of deciding to.

They sat silently in the windowless storage closet turned office, under the buzz of the fluorescent lights.

"Knock knock," says a college-aged woman standing in the doorway. "Where's Mr. Wilson?"

"Who?" Zane asks.

"You're sitting in his office, silly," she says.

"Oh. He ran to the john."

"Ah, well, here are the sandwiches," she says, placing the three wrapped sandwiches on the desk. "I assume not all three are for him."

She winks at them and leaves. Zane and Brandon haven't eaten in twelve hours. Lured by the smells of the hot sandwiches wafting through the air, they opt not to wait for the guard to return.

"Chow down!" Clayton booms when he comes back and sees they've eaten half of their sandwiches already. "Boy, this looks good," he says, unwrapping his. "So, listen, I've got some good news. I made a phone call while I was sitting in the oval office, and, Zane, if you're willing to stick around while we sort this out, I've got the big fella an escort. Plenty of time to get him to and fro, plus the airport is small, and a half-hour lead time will be fine, if it comes down to that. Comply?"

"That's fantastic," Zane says, putting his hand on Brandon's shoulder, more relieved for his buddy than disappointed to be left behind. "I guess I'll write down the address for you now since you won't be getting it out of him later."

A second guard appeared at Clayton's office door, Brandon's escort.

"Looks like this is it," Zane says, painfully struggling to his feet, gesturing for Brandon to stand as well. "Take care of yourself, brother. Don't be a stranger." He gives Brandon a hug, standing on his tiptoes to get his arms around the giant's neck, lingering not only because he doesn't know if he'll see him again, but also because returning to his flat feet will hurt. "Don't forget the rest of your sandwich."

Brandon gives Zane's back a thud with his palm and leaves the office, following the second guard's gestures.

No surprise, Brandon is bigger than the guard. They go outside and get in an SUV, similar to Clayton's. Brandon remembers that he's supposed to knock his escort out. But when the guard starts the engine, Brandon notices two more men sitting behind him in the backseat.

"You know," the driver says. "Someone as dark as you sticks out like a sore thumb around here."

Back inside, Zane finishes his sandwich.

"Tell me about your cousin's family," Clayton says. "What did you do all evening?"

"We had dinner, and just talked," Zane says, quickly reminding himself of everyone's names. "Danielle recited some poetry she'd written, and I wrestled with the boys before they went to bed."

"The boys?"

"Yeah, Reese and Lyle. Lyle is the little one. Spunky little kid."

"The boys," Clayton repeats. "And after they went to bed?"

"Just talked to Melissa and Steve for a while. Nothing in particular. Just catching up."

"Which of them is your cousin again?"

"Melissa. I've never gotten to know Steve very well before tonight."

"Got it. How do you and the big fella know each other?"

"We grew up together," Zane says, relieved to mix some truth in with his lies. "Went to school together. I don't remember not knowing him."

"You called him brother a minute ago, but you're not actually related, right?"

Zane gauges the seriousness in Clayton's expression. Besides the extreme difference in size, he and Brandon differ in the color of their hair, eyes, and skin. "Not related," he says with a smirk, having decided the guard was joking.

Clayton smiles in return. "So, wrestling around with the boys, Lyle, and, uh, Reese, huh. That sounds rough."

Zane laughs. "It was a workout. I'm going to be sore tomorrow, that's for sure."

The guard leans back in his chair and loosens his belt to aid his shaky digestion.

"Well, make yourself comfortable," he says, putting his feet up on his desk and closing his eyes.

Recognizing the long haul he's in for, Zane leans back, too. Anxious, he entertains fantasies of Brandon's freedom in lieu of subconscious dreaming amid the occasional distant footsteps and clatter from elsewhere in the complex and the hum of the light fixtures. He dozes off anyway, however, and is wakened by the loud ringing of the phone on the guard's desk. Clayton's feet slide off the desk, taking some papers with it, and groggily he answers the phone.

Zane glances at the clock and sees that an hour has passed. He straightens himself in his chair and rubs his eyes. Clayton says little into the phone, listening instead.

"Bad news, Zane," Clayton says after hanging up, now fully alert. "Your buddy got to the hotel, but he was arrested before getting to the airport."

Zane's heart begins to pound. He swallows hard, aware of how wide his eyes have gotten but unable to adjust them.

The guard clicks the mouse on his computer, and Zane hears his own voice say, "I was given a code, but I can't remember it now. Can you let us out?"

"Where are you coming from?" the intercom voice, Clayton's, replies.

"We were at the Millers."

"See, you *did* say Millers," Clayton says. "That wasn't a bad guess, actually. There is a Miller here, but only one. Keith Miller. He's eighty-six. I don't know him very well, to tell you the truth."

Zane forces a shrug.

"By the way, that was my daughter earlier," he continues. "The girl who brought you your sandwich. She's back from college for the summer, and I got her a job here. Her name is Reese," he says, watching Zane's reaction. "Those damn unisex names. I hadn't anticipated any confusion when we settled on naming her Reese; naïve of me. But there's no confusion with her siblings' names. Danielle and Lyle. Lyle is the youngest, you got that right, but he's not a *little one*, as you referred to him earlier. No, he's seventeen, and already taller than me."

Zane would not have wrestled with someone taller than the guard, that's for sure, bad leg or no.

"And as for *Mr.* Wilson," Clayton says, and stops. Zane bows his head as he recalls that the coffee shop girl had referred to the guard as Mr. Wilson earlier; he'd been too distracted by the arrival of the sandwiches to notice. "Looks like you're putting the pieces together," the guard says. "Clayton was my great-grandmother's maiden name, which became her first son's middle name, which continues to be passed down. I am Stephen Clayton Wilson the Third. I've been called Clayton since I was born, though, to avoid confusion with my father. My parents gave me hell when we named our son Lyle instead of Stephen Clayton the Fourth."

The guard clicks a few more times on his mouse, and turns the computer monitor around to face Zane. "Here's the full video," he says.

The video is of the main gate. With a night vision filter on the camera, Zane watches the boosted Nissan hatchback roll up to the gate, and he watches Brandon first get out of the car, and then himself. The camera zooms in and he sees pretty clearly the incorrect keypad codes he'd tried. He watches himself lie to the voice on the intercom, followed shortly by Brandon's attempts to heave the bag over the fence.

"Heck of a score," Clayton says. "That bag is here, by the way, a few rooms down the hall. The officer who fished it out of the bushes got a horrible scrape across his face. Poor guy. But we forgive you for that. Anyway, I'm sure you can guess what we want to know next."

Zane can guess.

"Yes, this is quite the jam you guys have gotten yourselves into," the guard goes on. "And what incredible luck that of all the names in the directory, you picked mine. Otherwise, you're not a bad liar. So. Who's the bag going to?"

Tears flirt with Zane's eyes as he stares at his shoes, thinking about Brandon, who is as good as dead. Zane will give up everything, but it will take time.

"Yup," the guard continues. "Quite the jam."

FROM THIS TREE I HANG

SOMEHOW I'VE ALWAYS figured I'd go down like this. But then the sheriff rushes in and hollers, "hold everything!"

"Praise be to God," the sap next to me blubbers. "I'm not supposed to be here, you know."

But I see Dusty standing in the back, calm and in control, pompous smirk on his mug, and I realize he's behind the sheriff's calling a halt to the ceremonies.

The crowd oohs and aahs as the sheriff explains he's gotten a telegram and it turns out I'm innocent. The crowd don't like the "innocent" part. They never met me, but they'd turned out to see a hangin', and the bounty on my head is too high to be a mistake. The noose is loosened, anyways, though, and my hands are untied. The crowd voices its displeasure.

The sap next to me cries, "No, me! What about me?!"

I wink at the sap as my neck is freed from the rope. He spits on my shirt. But that don't bother me. I wump him on the shoulder and jump off the platform.

The sheriff grabs my arm. "You best hurry up and get out of here. I'm not gonna kill you, but *they* might, and you'd deserve it, too."

But wallowing in the crowd's outrage is too much fun. I stretch my arms to the sky and slowly turn all the way around so everyone can get a look at my innocent ass. They call me names, curse my dead mother, and throw fistfuls of sand and pebbles at my face. They spit, too, like the sap did, but they miss as often as they hit.

To divert attention away from me, the platform trapdoor is thrown, and the sap loses his footing. But no one pays mind, and the sap strangles unnoticed. Dusty shoves his way through the mob and grabs me by the collar. Over the mob noise, he shouts, "What the hell is wrong with you?" and pulls me away from the excitement. Behind me, the sap gags in desperation. As the mob grows ornerier, the sheriff doesn't move from the side of the platform. He's content to let them take the law into their own hands, and ready to turn his back if things get out of hand. But it don't get that bad before Dusty drags me out of harm's way and we ride off in a cloud of dust.

BUT DUSTY CAN'T BLACKMAIL the sheriff this next time. The sheriff and the preacher's wife have been found out, and he's been run out of town. The preacher's gone, too, disgraced, and guilty by association.

Everyone's yelling at me again, jeering, calling me names. It's worse than before because I got away. They're intent on seeing I ain't getting away again. And with that last sap underground, it's just me this time. The rope is tighter this time, too. All I can do is hope Dusty's around again somewheres with an ace up his sleeve.

Someone starts shooting off a ways. I crane my neck to try to spot him. It's Crazy Abe, a crack shot crackpot. Dusty and I met him a few days ago, stumblin' upon the aftermath of a raid. He took a likin' to us, but what he's doing shooting at the sky, I don't know, and everyone's screaming and falling to the ground or running away.

Except one person, who's standing around like nothing out of the ordinary's going on. It's Dusty! Not yelling, not running, he's simply watching Crazy Abe shoot holes in the heavens. The deputies crawl on their bellies and elbows to get close enough to Crazy Abe to take him down. Someone sneaks up behind him and conks him on the head. Crazy Abe spins around and shoots even more wildly than before. There's a mob closing in on him and next thing I know Dusty is in front of me hacking away at the rope above my head.

"Behind you!" I shout.

Someone has caught on and is rushing us. Dusty whips around and shoots him next to the star on his chest. He falls backwards. Crazy Abe must be dead by now. Dusty finishes with the rope and I fall to my knees, rubbing the rope burn on my neck.

"Let's never come back here," Dusty says as he grabs me by the hand and we run to where he's got the horses stashed.

DUSTY CONVINCES ME that we should lay low for a bit, and we head to his mama's farm. I ain't seen her in years. She never liked me much. I see her remembering how much she don't like me, for a few seconds, before she reluctantly greets me with a hug.

There ain't no adventure here. We get stuck diggin' up potatoes and carrots. After a bit I spot one of the farmhands sitting on the ground, leaning against a post. "Ain't you gettin' paid for this?" I complain. "What am I doin' in the dirt if you're just sittin' there? I don't get nothin' for sweatin' in the dirt."

I hear Dusty's mama tell him that she'd feed him three meals a day if he'd stick around. He would always have a roof over his head at night. And he can settle down with a nice girl and take over the farm; he don't even need to wait for her to die. She keeps bringing up this girl named Clara. Me and Dusty used to put worms down her dress when we was kids. Dusty's mom wants him to marry her, and I gather Clara's interested, too.

She's so happy Dusty's home that she draws him a bath. I can't even remember the last time I had a bath, so I hop in first when no one's looking, getting the water before Dusty mucks it up. Dusty sits next to the tub while I soak off the months of gunk and grime. He looks longingly at the water and at me, and admits he has no interest in marrying Clara, the girl we tormented all those years ago, but that he wouldn't mind sticking around the farm a while longer.

"I ain't stickin' around," I say.

"Well, now, you don't have to, but I wish you would," he says. The dirt freed from my skin floats on the surface of the bathwater. Dusty sticks his fingers in the water and swirls it around.

His mama sends us out to fetch a chicken for dinner. I say she should do it herself, but Dusty drags me outside and I watch him scoop up a chicken that gets too close. He twists its neck until its bony feet stop flailing in the air. He hands the chicken to me and tells me to start plucking; he's going to feed the ones he didn't kill. So I start plucking, one feather at a time.

"This is woman's work!" I say, throwing the dead bird back at Dusty.

She's trying to turn him into a farmer, Dusty's mom is, but we're outlaws, me and him, and always have been. She used to cry every time Dusty and I got into trouble when we was boys, but me and him was just answering our callings. She forbade him to see me back then, not that that ever stopped us. She feeds me good now, so much stew and bread that it feels sinful, but I can tell she'd rather I warn't around. She won't kick me out, though, afeard I'll take Dusty with me if she does.

But I hear them talking about it, and I know I gotta convince Dusty otherwise, before he gets all domesticated-like.

"What are we doing here?" I complain to him. "I don't wanna do this no more."

At this moment, what I don't want to do is to be milkin' cows before the sun is even up. Dusty shakes me pretty hard to wake me in the morning. I didn't ask for no bed, nor ain't it my fault a bed is more comfortable than the ground. And I never got kicked by no cow before comin' back here, neither. When they're full of milk, they's supposed to be uncomfortable, so if I'm milking them and making them feel better, what do they kick for?

"We got no place else to go," Dusty says.

"That never stopped us before. You don't want to be tied down somewheres."

"I'm thinking of stickin' around." He's finally out with it. "Mama needs lookin' after. And she can pay one less farmhand with me around."

"Now looky here, she's turning you against me!" I accuse him. "She wants you to marry that stupid girl!" I yank hard on an utter, too hard, and get a groan from the cow.

"I don't want to marry no girl," he says. "I only want you to stick with me."

"This ain't no way to live," I say, gesturing toward the open end of the barn where you can see the rising sun behind the farmhouse and the gardens. "We was living real lives before, and I aim to get back to it. And you're comin' with me."

I kick over my milk bucket. It warn't a quarter full but the contents spill out anyways. I huff out of the barn to gather my things, leaving Dusty behind. But I know he'll follow. His mama cries when we head out, and he cries some, too. I'll chide him for that later.

NOW EVERYBODY'S DEAD, and that includes the lynch mob that was after us. I recognize some of the faces that had yelled at me before, eyes now looking up at me wide and lifeless, skin blistering in the sun, blood-soaked shirts topped with dust and flies. Last time I saw them their eyes were full of fire. The sheriff is over there, the ex-sheriff, now the dead sheriff. Maybe he talked them into this.

The sheriff had it out for me, of that I'm sure. But it warn't me that squealed on him for sleeping with the preacher's wife. We busted in on him with her, yes, but he bought us off to keep us quiet and we honored the deal. It warn't our fault everyone found out anyways and runned him out of town. The preacher packed up and left, too, but he headed in the opposite direction, from what I heard.

Dusty's down there, the poor devil. It might've been him after all who told on the sheriff, now that I think about it. But if so, I don't know why. Dusty put up a good fight today, sneakin' up on foot; they didn't hear him until he was breathing down their necks. He just about pulled it off, too, getting everybody, but not before they got him, too. He crawled towards me, to my horse, and grabbed the stirrup.

"Help me, Dusty," I said. "Get off your sorry ass and cut me loose!"

But he was too weak to stand. He lost his grip of the stirrup and his arm thumped to the ground. Looking up at me he said, "Sorry." But the good Lord only allowed him one last breath. Sorry for bungling the rescue, I figure he meant. Well, I'm sorry, too.

Sorry because I will most surely hang to death this time, from this tree, miles from civilization, feet dangling two feet above the ground. They had me tied up, sitting on a horse, and they was 'bout ready to whip its ass out from under me when Dusty showed up.

But instead we sat there, the horse and me, all afternoon, till the horse got thirsty or hungry, or just plain bored, and pulled out from under me, and trotted away.

PROWLER

TROY HEARS THE PROWLER, its wheels on the gravel, before he sees it. He is reading a James Lee Burke novel on the front porch and rocking back and forth on his rocking chair. Looking up he sees the prowler pull into his driveway. His heart still skips a beat at the sight of police on his property, even though the business from several years ago has now largely been forgotten around town.

Out of the prowler steps his old classmate, Sheriff Margaret.

"Mornin', sheriff," Troy says. He finds it unnatural to call her that, albeit amusing, and he stifles a smile. Margaret detects this in his address.

"Troy," she replies. "Your wife home?"

"Want me to fetch her?"

She shakes her head. "Not necessary."

He finds it hard to believe that someone so for-get-able, as Maggie had once been, was now the sin-gular person of authority. They'd grown up together in their small town and attended a school that had only one class per grade. For thirteen years, from kindergarten through twelfth grade, Troy and Maggie had spent thousands of classroom hours together, but without really getting to know each other. It hadn't been until the investigation a few years back, when Maggie, then only a deputy, had been coming around all the time, that they'd had their first in-depth conversations.

Reluctant to stop reading, Troy keeps the Burke open but lays it face down. "Did Old Man Sanders call you about his mailbox?" he asks. His neighbor a skip down the road came home yesterday from a three-day trip to find his mailbox and its contents scorched, with the remains of some fireworks discernible.

"He did," Sheriff Margaret says. "In fact, they lit up three mailboxes this week."

"Boy, I'd love to catch 'em in the act," Troy says, imagining what he'd do to someone tampering with his own mailbox.

"So would I," the sheriff says. "All summer there have been reports of petty vandalism. They're defecating on driveways and in unlocked cars and unloading cans of shaving cream through open windows. They hang out of the window of a moving car, grab hold of a garbage tote and drag it down the street alongside the car before letting it fly, spewing garbage everywhere. They're even shaving animals."

"Shavin' animals?" Troy laughs.

"Well, just one so far," Maggie admits. "Mrs. Whiting's poodle. If you thought it was ugly before, you should see it now."

"Reckon I'll swing by and check it out," Troy says, laughing again, and Maggie too permits herself a chuckle.

With only so many girls in class, it had been inevitable that Troy would go out with some of them. Actually, he went out with all of them—went out with most of the girls in the class behind him as well—except Maggie.

This hadn't occurred to him until years later. And it had been Courtney, one of his high school flings and his current wife, who had brought it to his attention while poring through an old yearbook. Why not Maggie? She'd been attractive enough, he supposed, looking at her picture; not gorgeous but prettier than some. But weekend after weekend he had taken other girls to the drive-in, to the rodeo, or to Wednesday night square dancing, and weekend after weekend it had never been her.

Courtney used to laugh and say that Maggie was a dork. But while Troy didn't remember high school Maggie very well, he didn't think he would've had a problem dating a dork.

"Folks gettin' anxious for you to figure out who's doin' it?" he asks.

"I know who's doing it," Sheriff Margaret says, "at least some of them. Just no proof yet."

Her attention shifts to Troy's property, and she gazes around. During the investigation, Troy and Courtney had nervously joked that she was getting to know their land better than they knew it themselves. Maggie didn't come around much anymore, but you could tell she hadn't let it go.

"Well," she says, as if she feels she shouldn't have to ask. "Anything unusual going on around here?"

"Not that I've noticed."

"Would Courtney have noticed anything?"

"She'd tell me."

"Mind if I poke around a bit?"

Troy sticks a scrap piece of paper inside the Burke to close it up, stands, and sets the book on the rocking chair.

"Why not," he says, stepping off the porch to join her. "Smoke?" he says, pulling a cigarette out for himself.

Maggie shakes her head and says, "I'm quitting," as they step off the driveway onto the grass and slowly walk along the side of the house. Troy thinks he sees Courtney's shadow in the window.

"Quittin', but not yet quit?"

"I've quit a dozen times, but it's never took. Now I'm quitting. I'll say I've quit once it sticks."

"You gain weight?" he asks.

"You shouldn't ask a woman that."

Maybe not. But he can't tell. He thought maybe she was a little big-boned, as he had in mind Native Americans tended to be. Later he learned that wasn't actually true about Native Americans. Then he learned that she wasn't Native American at all, but half-Chinese. Weird that he hadn't been able to tell the difference. Courtney told him he was racist, but he was probably just an idiot.

"Courtney gained twenty pounds when she quit a few years ago," he offers. "It pissed her off so much she took it back up."

"I don't remember that," Maggie says.

"You warn't back yet."

Frustrated by not advancing in her own department, as well as by her colleagues' haphazard investigation of Troy and Courtney, she'd taken a position several counties over. Sometime later she was persuaded to come back, coaxed with the title of "acting sheriff," to take over for her recently dismissed former boss. Eventually the "acting" part of her title was dropped. She'd been gone four years.

"I've gained weight," she admits. "But I'll deal with it."

Troy's not surprised that she heads for the well. Many a morning, years back, he had wakened to the sight, out the back window, of Deputy Maggie staring down that well. Those were unsettling times. He remembers vividly the night that, fearing a warrant was forthcoming, he had gotten Courtney's brother to lower him down into the well to retrieve the remaining bits of evidence. The strap had broken, and Troy had plunged feet first into the water. In the dark water, within the narrow circumference of the stone walls of the well, he had panicked. His brother-in-law had dangled down an unbroken stretch of rope, and Troy had been able to grab ahold of it and climb the walls of the well with the recovered bits in his pocket before collapsing on the grass just as Maggie's prowler was pulling onto their property.

It had been night, and the deputy hadn't seen him. He bolted for the trees. From the distance he watched his former classmate talk to Courtney and her brother halfway between the well and the house. Luck showered upon Troy as it began to rain heavily. After an appropriate amount of time, he emerged from the back, looking wet from the precipitation. Maggie had not yet obtained a warrant, he learned.

Troy hadn't seen her on his property since she'd returned as sheriff, at least not without a preamble. And even then she'd seemed to have given up on the well.

But now, as she peers over the side to look into the depths, she is refocused. Standing behind her, Troy could easily push her in. Nothing to it, really. And thus the only person who still cared about his past would become the past. But how long would it take for her to drown? And how much yelling would she do in the meantime? And probably nobody was looking, but how can you know for sure? Plus, there would be the prowler to dispose of...

"Seems a likely spot to tamper with," she says. "If they'd been here."

She turns to look Troy in the eyes. He smiles.

"It does," he says agreeably.

She steps away from the well and heads deeper into the back. The next major landmark is the outhouse. Troy and Courtney had installed indoor plumbing upon buying the property, but they'd never taken down the outhouse.

"You ever use this thing?" Maggie asks.

"Rarely," Troy answers.

"But you do occasionally?"

"Some," he allows.

She flips the flimsy wooden latch of the outhouse to open the door, peer inside, and shine a light down the larger of the two holes.

"I wouldn't think it'd be much of a task to knock it down and fill it up."

"No, it wouldn't."

Troy looks behind him at the house to try to spot Courtney, but with the glare of the rising sun on the windows he can't see anything. With the outhouse door still open, he flicks his cigarettes through the hole before latching the door again.

They walk farther back, the grass and weeds suddenly longer, through the part of his many acres that he only occasionally mows. Maggie lives with her mother, Troy knows, and he wonders if she resents his having a house of his own. After high school, he had worked odd jobs for several years, never sticking to anything for more than a few months at a time. Every year or so he would run into Courtney, whom he'd briefly dated in high school, and they'd reconvene for a fling. Finally he knocked her up, they got married, and he considered starting a career. But when she lost the baby, he lost any sense of urgency about getting a job. The two of them continued floating carefree through life until Troy inherited a large sum from an uncle who had retired to Florida and hadn't seen what a loser his nephew had turned into. This house wasn't much to look at, but at least it was his.

Maggie, meanwhile, had been in JROTC in high school, had spent four years in the Army, and had then promptly joined the force. Other than tending to a garden and occasionally manning a produce stand along the side of the highway, Troy and Courtney didn't do anything, in Maggie's eyes.

"I swear, Troy, I don't know what's going on with kids these days," she says now. "Teachers can't punish a kid without a group of parents getting all up in arms. As if a kid can do no wrong. And so they grow up entitled, like they deserve whatever they want and don't have to do anything to get it."

As they trudge through the back half of the property, her speech takes on a lazy but unsettling rhythm. Someone else might have asked, at some point, where his property ended. But Maggie knows the property line even better than he does.

Her hair is in a ponytail today, but he remembers that she used to wear her hair in braids. "That's why I thought she was Native American," he had said to Courtney, to which she simply uttered the word "racist" again.

"What can ya do?" he says now.

"I'll arrest these brats, and then mommy will cry about how we're destroying their futures because of standard teenage immaturity and the judge will let them off with a slap on the wrist." She looks at him. "Y'all get away with everything."

"We're the same age, Maggie," Troy says. "You and me."

She disregards that and instead, pointing off aways, says, "what's that?" He can't tell exactly what it is from the distance, but indeed there's a foreign lump at the edge of his property line. They keep walking at a steady pace, but with each step the mass becomes clearer. They don't stop until they are five feet away.

The cow lies on its side and is decorated like a porcupine with more than a dozen arrows sticking out of it. It doesn't smell rotten, nor has it yet been scavenged, so it was likely killed overnight.

"Who has cows?" Sheriff Margaret asks.

"James has a few," Troy says, pointing in one direction, and then, pointing in the other direction, "I don't know his name, but the fella over yonder has some, too."

She shakes her head. "I told that damn school an archery team was a bad idea. They better shut that program down after this."

"But now this is a felony!" Troy says, perhaps too excitedly.

"Burning the mail was already a felony, but yes."

She takes several pictures of the cow and the arrows and they turn back toward the house, faster now. She doesn't say anything, and Troy knows well enough to stay silent.

"I'll be back shortly," Margaret says when they're back at the front of the house.

She gets into the prowler and Troy steps back onto the porch. He sees the Burke on his rocking chair, but his mind is too frazzled to concentrate on reading. He pulls out another cigarette, lights it, and takes a long drag before stepping inside the house.

Courtney too is smoking while looking out the window at the prowler where Margaret is making calls.

"What'd she want?"

"Some kids killed a cow back there," he says. "They shot the hell out of it with a bow and arrow."

"I saw her lookin' down the well again."

"She was just lookin' for an excuse to snoop around," he says. "Like old times, 'til she found the cow."

They stand in the hazy smoke and watch Maggie back the prowler out of the gravel driveway and cruise off.

"It's been years," he says, putting his left arm around her waist while taking a drag with his right. "We're fine, baby."

"Don't call me baby."

He pulls his arm away and smashes the cigarette in the nearest ashtray. Maybe he'll quit. He's never tried before.

"I can call you baby if I want," he says. "It's your goddam fault."

SANCTUARY

JODY'S HOME had been a revolving door of pregnant teenagers throughout his childhood. The girls had spent a lot of their time in his backyard, not necessarily *with* him, though he was often in the backyard as well, in his treehouse, sneaking occasional glances, his imagination running wild.

It had gradually been occurring to Jody that there was more going on than met his eleven-year-old eyes. In books he read, characters often discovered that their parents had dark secrets, and he couldn't help studying his parents with this in mind, looking for signs of unrest, wondering what was going on in the background that they hid from him. His parents had previously seemed united concerning the sanctuary they were providing pregnant teenagers, but now he sensed that his mother had become uncomfortable with it.

"He's at that age, Warren," he heard her say to his father. "He'll be looking at these girls differently, if he isn't already. He's starting to understand where all these babies are actually coming from."

"He's always known where they come from," his father said. "Every child knows babies come from their mother's tummies."

"But they don't know *how* they get there," his mother hissed. "They don't even wonder."

"He'd learn one way or another," his father argued. "Would you rather he learns from the boys in the locker room? It's better coming from me."

It had been just this past spring, at the tail end of fifth grade, that his father had sat Jody down for a fascinating, exciting, and somewhat mortifying lecture about the impending changes in his body and the general facts of life. Of course, Jody wasn't blind. He'd always been aware of the physical differences between adult men and adult women—he swore he could remember being breastfed—and even among kids his own age he'd seen the sprouting changes in his female classmates, some of whom he'd known since kindergarten. Still, learning about the *process* had been eye-opening.

"It must've been torture for Percy," his mother bemoaned, "all these years. That's obvious now. I never gave it any thought. And now he's gone!" And with this Jody could hear his mother weep and whack her husband in his chest with her fists.

Jody had wanted to be like Percy. Even as he came to realize how little he knew about older people, Jody was confident in Percy's goodness. While his friend Tommy's older brother had once gotten arrested for throwing rocks at a vacant building, Percy had been class valedictorian and had gone on mission trips with the church youth group. That seemed like a long time ago, even though the graduation ceremony had been only last month.

Jody peeked out of his treehouse at the new girl, Isabella, sitting by the pool. He zeroed in on her belly. He knew she was pregnant because why else would she be here, but she wasn't showing through her clothes. They always arrived this way, and their bellies always grew over the course of their several months' stay. He wondered if Isabella had brought a bathing suit.

The girls tended to be shy, reserved, and embarrassed, like the last girl, Rebecca. Isabella was not. In the backyard last week, when she'd first arrived, she'd called him over to ask his name and how old he was. Percy was more polite and had grown friendly with Rebecca, but Jody had been so rattled by the forwardness of this new pretty girl that he'd run inside the house.

"What were you and Rebecca talking about out there?" his mother had once asked Percy. Jody was grateful that his parents didn't have the wherewithal to realize that just because he wasn't in the room, he might not be listening around the corner.

"Life," Percy said after a moment's thought. "Plans for the future."

"That's interesting," his mother said. "What does Rebecca want to do with her life?"

"She's figuring things out," Percy replied.

His mother had smiled politely—how vividly Jody remembered that smile—and seemed not to consider it a sign of things to come. Who knew what was said out of his earshot, but he didn't think Percy was ever warned to stop talking to Rebecca.

What Jody knew was that even though these girls were pregnant, none of them were married. They came here through one of his church's ministries. Families provided sanctuaries for girls in crises where the girls would get through their pregnancies free of scorn and humiliation, until the babies were born and given up for adoption. Sometimes the girls came back from the hospital for a few days, suddenly much thinner, but sometimes they went straight back to their homes on the other side of the country, where their parents had been telling people they'd been abroad living with an aunt in Switzerland for the previous six months. This had been going on Jody's entire life.

"How do they get pregnant if they're not married," Jody once asked his older and wiser brother.

Percy looked at him piously, ruffled his hair, and said, "you'll learn about that when you're a little older, kid."

A little older had arrived. It was incredible that Percy had known all the things his father had told him presumably since *he'd* been eleven years old. It made him admire Percy even more for keeping it to himself.

But it also made him look at women differently: the girls in his class, yes, but also older women, his friends' mothers, his own mother, and the pregnant teenagers who came one at a time to stay with his family.

His father had stressed a few things. One was that sex was sacred and not to be taken lightly. Another was that he, Jody, should not make jokes about sex, that it was disrespectful to women, even if there weren't any women around. And third, that sex wasn't solely for the purpose of procreation, but was a benefit of marriage, a gift from God, and to be enjoyed by both the man *and* the woman.

His mother had *enjoyed* it? His friend Tommy's mom had *enjoyed* it? Rebecca had *enjoyed* it? And now that Rebecca was gone, Isabella had *enjoyed* it?

He tried to imagine the act, in his mind, he and a girl, or better yet someone else and a girl with him sitting off to the side to observe. First you did this, then you did that, then this went in there. How weird!

And yet, as he snuck a peek at Isabella sitting by the pool, his heart started doing backflips as he pictured her in the act, and there was movement in his pants.

This had happened several times recently. It was a new sensation—and a distracting one—and when it happened he lost his ability to think about anything else, so he would retreat to his bedroom.

***

PERCY HAD GONE about everything with great consideration. He'd sent a letter from a mailbox on the other side of town two days ahead of time. He didn't want his parents to worry, but he also didn't want to leave a note on his pillow or on the refrigerator that might be discovered a few minutes after he'd left, when he'd be barely down the street. The mail came mid-afternoon, so, assuming the letter came on schedule, he knew that if he left first thing in the morning he would have a sizable head start before anyone realized he'd run off, but not so great that anyone would have started worrying yet.

"Your mother looks at me like I have horns growing out of my head," Isabella said.

"She's upset," Jody said. He had faced his fears and had learned to speak to Isabella in complete sentences.

"So it's not me?"

"Well," Jody said, shrugging. It was true that his mother was colder with Isabella than he'd seen her with anyone else. "It's because of the last girl. My brother ran away with her."

Isabella laughed. "That's where he went?! He actually fell in love with one of us poor distressed whores?"

Jody flinched. He didn't know what a whore was—he thought it had something to do with wearing too much makeup—but he knew it was a really bad word to call someone. It confused him that Isabella would call herself a whore, or that Rebecca might have been one, too.

"They want to get married," Jody said, moving on.

She laughed out loud, though it sounded fake to Jody. "That's stupid. How old are they?"

Jody wouldn't have known Rebecca's age if he hadn't overheard his parents talking about it in distress: "But she's only seventeen, they can't get married!"

Jody relayed this to Isabella who gave her fake laugh and repeated, "stupid."

"How old are you?" Jody asked Isabella after a moment. He'd gotten better at asking questions. He wasn't sure why he hadn't asked this one yet.

"Fifteen," she said.

"I'm eleven."

"I would've guessed younger."

His bravest question was asking who the father was. She had looked at him curiously but told him it was a boy named Trevor, her best friend's older brother—*former* best friend. He'd been home during spring break when she and her friend, his sister, had gotten into a huge argument, and he'd been there to console her.

"How old is Trevor?" Jody asked now.

She scoffed. "I know where this is going," she said, though Jody didn't know what she meant. "Twenty, all right? He's twenty, and I'm fifteen."

This didn't mean anything to Jody, but he said, "okay."

"My parents want to sue him, get him arrested for statutory rape."

Jody didn't know what that meant either. His father's speech had included biological and spiritual talking points, but otherwise had not addressed very many no-no's.

"They were all like, 'you're so young,' and I'm like, please, I knew what I was doing, you know? Trevor's so freaking pathetic, he wouldn't've touched me if I hadn't come on to him." She looked at the boy. "Why am I telling you this? You probably don't even know what I'm talking about."

"I do too!" Jody lied.

"Anyway, if they were following through with it, with the charges or whatever, I'd need to submit a statement, right? And I haven't. So poor Trevor can breathe deep and relax."

Jody decided to take his boldest leap yet. "That's good, but, um, like, how did, you know, how did the baby, uh, get in there?"

This was what he'd been pining to hear ever since his father had given him the talk: an account of sex from someone who was not his father. He'd been warned not to make jokes about it, but he wasn't making jokes.

Instead, he was having a serious discussion, an *educational* discussion, even.

Isabella looked at the little kid who was the only member of this household nice enough to keep her company. She'd been bored out of her mind. She remembered the kid's older brother; he'd been there when she'd first arrived, but they hadn't talked. Jody's father was a stiff, and his mother, cordial at first, had been treating her like a leper since Percy flew the coop.

"Ask your parents," she finally said.

"I mean," his face flushed. "I know how babies are made. Just..."

"You want to hear about the parts they left out?"

That was an interesting way to put it, he thought, and he nodded. Like, how do you even get into a position to *start*?

She scoffed again.

"Find me some cigarettes," she said, "and I'll tell you whatever you want to know."

JODY DIDN'T HAVE the first clue where to find cigarettes. His parents certainly didn't smoke. He didn't know *anyone* who smoked. He looked for cigarettes to steal in stores in the height of his desperation to hear Isabella's description of sex with Trevor, but cigarettes were always behind the counters. He kept his eyes open for packs of cigarettes that might've fallen on the sidewalk. Failing that, he resolved to be as good a friend as possible to her, the kind of friend someone would tell everything to.

"I really don't like Jody spending so much time with that tramp," he heard his mother hiss to his father.

"Please don't call her that," his father said, less quietly. "You know full well that girls lie about this kind of thing all the time. She's probably scared. How could you call her that?"

"She's not one of the nice ones. And after what happened with Percy…"

"Percy is eighteen. Jody is eleven. *Eleven*, for crying out loud."

"Eleven-year-olds do stupid things too."

Jody wasn't sure that what Percy had done was stupid. He was an adult now, old enough to vote, to join the military, to buy cigarettes. He wished Percy was here to buy him cigarettes to give to Isabella, although then maybe Isabella would tell Percy about sex instead of him.

Percy had written several letters to his parents. The return address wasn't a real address—123 Nothing St, Fake City, 54321—so his parents couldn't write back or track him down. His letters were naive, as if he imagined his parents might be all right with the fact that their oldest son had passed up a full college tuition scholarship to elope with a formerly pregnant refugee. They weren't legally married, of course, Percy acknowledged in his letters, but they were now married "in the eyes of God."

"By who?!" his mother cried. "What kind of quack preacher would marry an eighteen- and seventeen-year-old 'in the eyes of God'?!"

Jody's father went pale.

Jody relayed this new information to Isabella.

"Wow," was her reaction. "'In the eyes of God,'" she repeated. "Something tells me Rebecca and I would not be friends in real life."

"Do you think it's wrong?" Jody asked. "My mom is pretty upset. My dad, too, I guess."

"I don't know if it's wrong," Isabella said. "It's stupid, but." She shrugged. "Who says you have to go to college to make decisions for yourself?"

"Like you," Jody said. "You make decisions for yourself."

"What the hell does that mean?!"

"Well, you said, um, you and Trevor. It was your decision, not his."

"Oh." She shrugged. "Right."

"Did you ever think about running away?" Jody asked.

"Only a hundred times. *Everybody* thinks about it, sometimes."

Until now, Jody hadn't. Even when he'd read a book about someone running away, or a kid stranded in the wilderness of northern Alaska or on a deserted island, he'd get so anxious for his home and his parents that he'd disconnect himself from the character and situation.

"You wanna run away with me?" he asked.

"Sure," she said, deadpanned. "How about Friday?"

HE WAS EXCITED about this. Frankly, neither of his parents had been pleasant to be around this summer.

The week slogged on. He tried to pass the time by reading or riding his bike, but suddenly every day was *thirty*-four hours long instead of twenty-four. A man came to see Isabella a couple of times. Jody didn't know his name, but he knew he was a counselor from church. He always came to talk to the girls. Jody wasn't allowed in the backyard while they talked. He was there Friday morning, when Jody and Isabella were supposed to run off in the manner of Percy and Rebecca. Jody had already packed his bag. He planned to call from a gas station later that afternoon, because he'd forgotten to mail a letter the way Percy had.

When the counselor left, Jody went out the back-door, bag in hand, and confidently approached Isabella, who had her back to him.

"It's Friday," he said. She didn't move. "I'm sorry I haven't found any cigarettes for you." She scoffed. "I tried. Anyway, I'm ready to go if you are."

She finally looked his way, noticed the bag at his side, and remembered.

"I have to stay here until the baby is born," she said.

"Well," Jody began, because he'd thought of this. "I know I'm not that old, but I can be the dad. I mean, I can learn, right? You don't have to give it up. We can be the baby's mom and dad together."

"Raise the baby together?"

"Yeah," he smiled. "Why not? It would be fun."

She shook her head in exasperation.

"I don't want to keep it," she said. "I don't *want* to. You think I want a constant reminder of what that piece of shit did to me? I'd jam a coat hanger in there, stab the fetus in the eye, and pull it out if I had the guts."

Jody shuddered at the imagery. "What he did to you?" Jody asked. "Trevor? I thought you said it was you."

She stared at the water, at the pool she hadn't gone into even once, her jaw clenched.

"No one wants that kind of attention," she muttered.

Jody still didn't understand. Isabella's eyes glanced at him, and she saw his expression.

"My God, you're the stupidest kid I've ever met. You live here, for crissakes. Don't you know what this place is?"

Jody still stared blankly, clueless.

"Girls get raped all the time. But no one wants to go through life labeled a rape victim and have people whisper about them as they walk by. And you sure as hell don't want to keep the baby. Why would we? So it's either get an abortion or give it up for adoption. Someone else can take the baby. Then Trevor can finish college, I'll go back to school, and hopefully no one will be none the wiser."

She glowered, and after a moment, Jody said, "so Trevor is bad?"

Isabella sighed. "Trevor is bad."

"And you didn't enjoy it?"

She rolled her eyes and said, "No, I didn't enjoy it." She sighed again. "It was the worst day of my life."

He couldn't believe he'd been looking at her wrong all this time. And if she hadn't enjoyed it, then Rebecca probably hadn't, either. Had Trevor enjoyed it? And hadn't his father told him that it was supposed to be enjoyable for both the man *and* the woman?

"Can you get out of here, kid? I really don't want to talk to you anymore."

Jody backed away. He would look up the word "rape" in the dictionary later, but for now he climbed into his treehouse to cry in the corner.

INVOLVEMENT

AT THE BAR I ASK whether we, as college professors, should friend our students on Facebook, or, more specifically, whether we should accept friend requests from our students. I don't want to be more involved than I have to be with my students' personal lives. But I also don't want to be the only square in the music department who closes himself off from the student body. Joseph says that if I don't accept their friend requests I will miss out on some "classic shit." Kristen points out I won't be able to tell "if they're lying about being too sick to go to classes."

I learn of Elliot's broken engagement from one of his posts:

The degree of pain and heartache I am feeling is inhumane...

which a week later continues with:

Is there something inherently unlikable about me? What is it that makes people turn around when they see me...

before eventually he admits defeat by downgrading his relationship status to:

it's complicated

I consider asking Sandra why she dumped Elliot, as it is obviously she who did the dumping. I run into her at the local music store when I stop in to get ready for the upcoming semester. I've never seen her happier. But I don't ask her anything. I don't want to be involved.

Elliot is one of my seniors. This is our first lesson in months, even though he promised he would take lessons over the summer. For three years he's been in and out as a performance major. Whenever he lost the faculty's approval he had to re-audition, and thus he kept re-entering and re-exiting the program, annoying almost everybody in the process. After his junior recital, which was technically optional as he was out of the program at the time, we decided to give him one more chance to prove us wrong.

And here we are, the first week of classes, I haven't seen him in months, and with the first few notes it's obvious he took most of the summer off. In a few days he is scheduled to play not only for me but also for the entire faculty who will then collectively decide whether he can graduate with a performance degree.

And he's crying, so I can't even yell at him.

"Can we put off Elliot's jury a little longer?" I ask my colleagues on his behalf.

Kristen laughs. "Isn't it tomorrow? He wants a stay of execution?"

"Why prolong the inevitable?" Joseph says, he our department chair, less amused than Kristen. "I personally have been looking forward to failing him all summer. Unless of course he's made leaps and bounds, and I'm talking Julliard quality."

"Yes, the jury is only a formality," Kristen agrees, laughing less, but still some, "to make his failure as a college student official. Breakups can be hard, but you can't let that get in the way of academic development."

"Unless he's got something on you," Joseph says, joining in on Kristen's fun. "Dirty pictures or an incriminating recording. What are you hiding, Dr. Bell?"

"One week?" I ask, ignoring them both, which is all it takes to get them to reschedule.

Elliot has always been annoying in a "no balls" sort of way. But at least he shows up to the hearing, which is more than he did yesterday for what should have been his second lesson since April. And at least he wears a tie. But he plays very few right notes. If there's anything more useless than an undergraduate performance degree, it's a non-specified bachelor of arts in music, which is what he will receive if I don't convince Joseph and Kristen to give him one final chance — for real this time — two weeks from now.

"HI, TYLER, HAVE you seen what lover boy posted today?" Kirsten asks me in the faculty lounge as I heat water for tea. "Your soaring senior?"

"Who? Elliot?" I ask. She shows me the screen of her iPhone, which is open to Facebook. "Why are *you* friends with him?" I ask.

She shrugs. "He was in my first-year seminar."

Is anybody looking for an engagement ring? I have one for sale.

"Oh, good God."

Kristen laughs. "This is usually when you make a joke about his balls."

"Have you looked behind the couch? Maybe they're back there."

"DO YOU EVEN WANT to graduate?" I ask.

"I'm sorry, I just have a lot going on right now…" Elliot says.

It has been more than four months since he began his online pity party. I've decided I will no longer allow it as an excuse.

"I can't pass you if you sound like you haven't picked up your trombone in a week. What's going on with you?" To ask this is an invitation into his private life, a mistake, but I recover by not giving him time to answer. "I don't want to make you write out a practice chart, like I do with my freshmen, but if that's what it will take then that's what we'll do."

"I'm sorry, it's just that I've been feeling…"

"Elliot, please, it's getting harder and harder to defend you. You realize the only reason you haven't failed yet is because of *me*. *I'm* the one sticking up for *you*. *You* would be a communications major if it weren't for *me*."

"I know, I'm sorry, Dr. Bell. It's just I've been going through a lot lately…"

"So I've read."

"…Plus I've got this ring I need to sell…"

"Yes, Elliot, I need to cut this short so I can get to a meeting I'm almost late for."

I sit back as I watch Elliot pack up slower than anyone has ever packed up a trombone in the history of the world. Finally he's at the threshold of the door. I stand up, too, and grab a random folder to authenticate my excuse.

"See you later, Dr. Bell."

"Take care, Elliot. By the way, how much are you asking for that ring?"

Dammit.

"I paid eighteen-fifty, but I'd take sixteen hundred. Are you interested?"

"No!" I almost shout. What's wrong with me? "See you later," I say, and I hurry down the hall to the meeting I've made up.

ELLIOT FAILS AGAIN. He plays better than last time, but based solely on this performance we probably wouldn't have accepted him into the performance program as an incoming freshman, let alone pass him as a senior. He seems content to receive the useless degree he's now officially set to receive. Kristen and Joseph would have taken more pleasure in failing him if they hadn't been expecting me to beg for a *final*-final chance for him. But I don't even bring it up. Nor does Elliot ask me to.

Then he gets into a car crash. The light turned green so he went. But he was second in line and the driver in front of him hadn't budged because of a jaywalking pedestrian.

"He's willing to settle privately, so the insurance companies don't get involved…" Elliot explains.

"Sounds like a man without insurance."

"…And I know that if I reported it my rates would raise for sure…" He'd had an accident last year, too, I now recall. "But if I do settle privately I'll have to ask my parents for money…"

I end up buying his engagement ring.

"I really can't go lower than fifteen hundred, Dr. Bell."

"That's fine, Elliot, you can keep it. I'm not paying fifteen hundred for something I don't even want."

"I paid eighteen-fifty, though, and…"

"Hold out for eighteen-fifty, then."

"Could you go fourteen, at least?"

"Elliot, please."

"Thirteen?"

"Oh, God."

"Twelve-fifty?"

I cave at a thousand and bring him cash the next day.

"I SAW SANDRA the other day while I was buying valve oil," Joseph says. "She said more during those two minutes than I've heard her say the last three years."

After sitting through another inglorious student recital, the three of us have gone out again, per custom. Kristen buys the first round and puts her hand on my arm when she sets my drink in front of me. I love it when she does this, but she does the same with Joseph, so I don't get excited.

"She's liberated," Kristen says. "Free from oppression."

"What are you implying?" I ask.

"Just that if Elliot had his way," Joseph says, "she would've spent their marriage chained to the radiator with just enough slack to reach the kitchen and the bathroom."

"Are you joking?" I ask.

"And the laundry room," Kristen adds.

"And eventually the nursery," Joseph says.

"And that at some point somebody told Sandra it's not 1950 anymore," Kristen continues.

"What?!" I say. "What are you basing this on?!"

Joseph starts to laugh and then chokes on his beer. Kristen whacks him on the back.

"She discovered what a useful thing the brain is, and that she'd like to use hers."

"And that she even had one in the first place!"

"Where are you getting this?!" I plead.

They both grin at me. "Forget we said anything," Kristen says.

"Right," Joseph agrees. "You don't want to be involved in your students' lives and we should respect that. I apologize for bringing it up."

They're laughing at me, and I don't understand why.

Needless to say, I look at Elliot differently the next time he's in my studio. I eye him closely as he plays his etude. He's a small and unintimidating guy. He doesn't look like a future wife beater. I'm going to tell Joseph and Kristen they don't know what they're talking about.

"That's sounding a lot better," I say. "Good improvement in general. You doing all right?"

"Well…" he begins.

Dammit.

"Keep up the good work, Elliot."

"…I'm going to need another five hundred dollars for the ring."

"You're kidding."

"I paid eighteen-fifty for it. I really can't go lower than fifteen hundred."

"But you did. You went lower. You took a thousand."

"I just need another five. It's still a good deal."

"Not for me. What am I going to do with it?"

"Propose to someone."

"Elliot," I say. "It's time to go. I'll see you next week."

AFTER OUR FACULTY meeting the next day I linger longer than usual. Finally I'm alone with Joseph, who, as the instrumental music chair, ran the meeting.

"What's up, Tyler," he says, as he finishes packing his briefcase.

"This kid, Elliot," I say.

"You know what, Tyler? You tried your best with that kid. You tried your ass off. We admire your dedication, honestly; Kristen and I were talking about it the other day; we really do. But it's a losing battle. Just go through the motions with him, and in a few months he'll be out of here, and if there's any justice we'll never see him again."

"I guess you're right."

"Those kids happen. They shouldn't, but they do. And Elliot was a freshman your first year teaching, right? Of course you're attached to your first class. I get it. But a kid like that, all you can do is tell him to grow a pair and kick his ass to the curb. Believe me, he's no reflection on you."

SOMETIMES I HAVE an appointment, a makeup lesson, and a faculty meeting in the same afternoon and it's not worth going home before the student recital that evening. But the practice rooms closest to my studio are filled with students so sitting alone in my studio during the six o'clock hour isn't as quiet as one might like. One of the practicing students is scheduled to perform in an hour. If you don't have it by now it's too late, I want to shout. But I'm not going to complain about a student practicing. A mixture of woodwinds, brass, and piano, it's easy to pick out my students by the sound of the instrument, their playing quirks, their mistakes. None of them are Elliot.

Someone knocks on my door and I go to answer. I smile in greeting the middle-aged couple.

"I'm sorry, you look familiar, but I can't quite place you."

"Mr. and Mrs. Deborg, Dr. Bell," the man says. "Elliot's parents."

Now my smile is forced, and I feel the ingenuity seeping through.

"What can I do for you?" I ask, and add, "Is Elliot all right?"

"Elliot is as good as anyone would be after being betrayed by his teacher and mentor." Mr. Deborg is taller than me, and therefore much taller than Elliot. He does the talking, while his wife hides meekly behind him.

"Betrayed?!" We have to speak loudly over the sounds coming from the practice rooms. "I have fought to give Elliot chance after chance and he has continuously let me down."

"You took advantage of a boy's vulnerability…"

"Boy? He's twenty-one!"

"…And you stole that ring from him for a fraction of its value."

"Stole?! A thousand dollars is nothing to sneeze at. And he practically begged me to buy it. What do I want with an engagement ring? I don't even have a girlfriend."

"It's worth almost twice what you gave him."

"Not to me. To me it's worth much, much less.

"Dr. Bell…"

"Look, he can have the ring back. I've got it in my car; I'll go get it. And then you can give me my grand back. That sounds good to me. Let's do that."

"He's got no use for an engagement ring."

"I've got no use for it!"

"Dr. Bell," Mr. Deborg talks down to me. "A deal is a deal…"

"Yes! That's right! It is!"

"But you didn't hold up to your end of the bargain. You owe Elliot five hundred dollars, and really, you should give him more, for the inconvenience."

We have an audience. The practice rooms are silent and the kids, maybe a dozen of them, have come out of their holes to watch the show.

I reach inside my studio for my coat, turn off the light, and close the door. Rather than commenting on the absurdity of their accusation, I say, "I'm leaving now."

I'm supposed to go to a recital in a little bit, part of my duties as a faculty member, to help determine whether a flute major will pass her senior recital and thus fulfill a requirement to graduate this December—

only one semester late—but I decide to go straight home instead. On my couch I watch the baseball play-offs and peruse my phone. I see that earlier in the day Elliot posted on Facebook:

I'm coming to grips with being betrayed by the people I trust the most.

Tomorrow, I decide, if Elliot doesn't give me my money back for his ring, I will go downtown and pawn it. I'll take a hit, I don't care, as long as I'm no longer responsible for it.

Kristen texts me, no doubt between recital pieces, calling me a wise man for sparing myself the torture of tonight's faux-virtuosic performance. Joseph texts later, after the recital would have ended, to say that a) the recital was one big pile of mediocrity but they're going to pass her anyway, and that b) there is a bizarre accusation going around about me of which he just got wind. I try calling him but he doesn't answer. He often leaves his phone in the car when we go to the bar. I consider joining him—Kristen is with him, I'm sure—but I'm still too freaked out to leave the house.

The next morning is my busiest teaching morning of the week. I'm in the zone two minutes into my first lesson and don't give Elliot a thought. I'm a little exhausted by noon, and when my last student leaves, I lean back at my desk and enjoy a sense of accomplishment.

"What the hell is going on?" Joseph says at the door, inviting himself in, and closing the door behind him. "Last night one of my students told me you conned that Elliot pansy out of the engagement ring Sandra gave back to him? They're saying it was a priceless heirloom and he was so desperate for cash that you took advantage of him and forced him to accept six hundred dollars for it? What the hell is wrong with you?"

"Family heirloom? He didn't even pay two grand for it."

"So the rest is true?!"

"No! Almost none of it is true!"

"Almost none?! Look, I know we give you a hard time about wanting to keep your distance from your students' personal lives, but that's actually a good rule to live by, so I would've hoped you weren't taking us seriously."

"Oh God, is that really what's going around?"

"Oh yeah," Joseph says. "Real shit storm. So guess what you and I are about to do?" I look at him blankly. "We're going to see the dean. He wants you in his office ay-sap. Like, now, if you're free."

"The dean?"

"As your chair I'm going to sit in on the meeting and defend you. But before we head upstairs you need to tell me with as much detail as possible what the hell is really going on."

My phone vibrates. It's Kristen calling me. I've received thousands of texts from her but I don't think she's ever actually called me. I wonder if she calls Joseph.

"I was leaving for an appointment when I saw that the side window of your car is shattered, and the door is wide open!"

"Oh no!" I shout, startling Joseph a good bit. I give him the abridged version and he says he's right behind me but I'm already down the hall, out the building, running for the parking lot.

"Hi, Dr. Bell!" I hear someone call.

I look over and see Elliot sitting on a bench.

"Hey buddy, you doing all right?" I say, not stopping to talk, but slowing down enough not to be rude. He's smiling, which is strange under the circumstances, but I haven't seen him smile in months so I welcome it. "Stay out of trouble, I'll catch you later."

"Tyler, I'm so sorry," Kristen says as I arrive at my car. "I wish I could stay and help but I'm running late. Let me know if there's anything I can do."

She touches my arm before getting in her car and driving off. I'm left staring at the shards of glass along the passenger side of my car. There have to be witnesses. It's not like the faculty lot is hidden. The sun was up when I arrived this morning. I can see students milling about from here. I can even see Elliot sitting on the bench, watching me. I look at the streetlights and trees, thinking there must be a security camera hidden somewhere. I'm mildly confident that whoever did this will be caught. Assuming it's a student, I hope he's expelled, or at least put on probation.

Then I remember something. I open the glove box, but the ring is gone.

"Ahh!" I loudly groan.

"Jesus, Tyler, I'm sorry," Joseph says, as he finally catches up. "What kind of an animal…is anything missing that you can tell?"

Just the evidence, I think to myself. Joseph puts his arm on my back and bends over to get a better look inside.

"Was there anything valuable?" he asks.

"I don't know," I mumble.

"You have insurance, I assume," he says. "Go ahead and call the police. I'll talk to the dean and we can do our thing later."

"What? Oh, the dean? Yes, let's do that later."

Joseph walks back towards the music building while I dial 9-1-1. I close the car door and, even though anyone with an arm could easily reach inside, I press the automatic locks. I turn to go sit next to my student while I wait for the cops to arrive. But Elliot isn't there anymore.

TABLE FOR TWO

NICK RAN THROUGH THE RAIN and through the restaurant's front entrance. He wiped the water from his face and grinned at the teenage hostess at the podium.

"Table for two," Nick said.

The hostess smiled back. "Are you meeting someone?" she asked.

"No, she's here; she forgot something in the car and had to run back."

"Are we waiting for her?"

He started to nod but changed his mind. "Nah, she'll find me."

"Right this way."

They twisted through the restaurant toward an empty booth. Nick sat down. The hostess placed two menus on the table, one in front of him and one on the other side.

"Your server will be right with you."

"Thank you."

He looked around the restaurant and gave a wide smile, so wide it was hard to tell whether he was smiling or frowning.

"Hello, I'm Carol. I'll be taking care of you this evening," said someone new standing over him at the head of the table. "What can I get you to drink?"

He started, caught off guard. "Oh, yes." He pointed to the empty chair opposite him. "She just ran to the car, forgot her phone. She's gotta have it." He let out a chuckle. "Water is fine for both of us."

"I'll give you a minute to glance over the menu, and I'll be back with two waters."

Nick forced the same smile as she walked off. He opened his menu and glanced through, locking eyes with an entrée. He nodded to himself. Then, leaving it open to the same page, he switched his menu with the menu across from him. He opened the other one, looked through it, nodded again, and left it in front of him.

Carol came back with two glasses of water and set them down on opposite sides of the table. "She's still not back?"

"That's bad timing!" Nick gave a laugh. "She ran to the bathroom, but we can order anyway. I'll have the New York strip, rare." He pointed to the open menu across from him. "She said she wants the house salad, dressing on the side. Italian."

"Great, I'll get your orders in."

"Thank you," Nick said as she walked away.

This was the type of restaurant teenagers went to on dates. He and Laura had come here on their first date during their high school senior year. He looked around at the nervous teenagers pretending to be adults. Through the windows he saw that the rain had let up and that the setting sun was reflecting off the puddles. At the bar, he saw his friends Brian and Sadie, presumably killing time before they headed for the movie theater. They hadn't spotted him yet.

Nick had been a groomsman in Brian and Sadie's wedding in July. Toward the end of the reception, when the bride threw her garter over her head into a sea of unmarried men, Nick had caught it. Whether Sadie had been aiming for him nobody knew, but it hadn't seemed like a fluke; everyone was pretty sure that Nick and Laura would soon be engaged. They were invited to Brian and Sadie's house for dinner a few weeks later, after Brian and Sadie returned from their honeymoon in Paris. The evening had been memorable, although they hadn't gotten together again since. Nick didn't take it personally. He knew that Brian's job kept him busy and that Sadie was finishing up pharmacy school. Nick was happy for them. They appeared to have a good life.

Nick took a sip of his water, and then a gulp. He kept drinking until it was half-empty. He switched the glass with the one across from him and drank until it too was only half-full. He left the glasses where they were.

The waitress came back with a plate and a bowl of salad. She set the salad in front of Nick and the steak across from him, but Nick didn't point out her mistake. He flashed his awkward smile, and she left without saying anything.

He ate several forkfuls of salad and a bread stick. He drank most of the water that was in front of him. He glanced around the restaurant before switching everything around. He cut into the steak. It wasn't rare, like he'd asked, but it was still plenty pink with a small splotch of red, and a little blood blended with the potatoes. He polished off the potatoes, sopping the blood as he went. When he'd eaten half of the steak, he leaned back to give the food a moment to digest. Then he switched everything around and continued his work on the salad.

"Nick!" Nick looked up to see Brian and Sadie at the head of his table.

"Hey man!" Nick stood up and gave Brian a hug. Then he gave Sadie a hug, her body language more reluctant than Brian's. "How are you, Sadie?"

"I'm all right, Nick, thank you," she said.

"We were on our way to catch a movie when we saw you sitting here," Brian said.

"Yes! Good. Laura and I are just enjoying a wet Friday date night. She's in the bathroom, not really feeling too well all of a sudden," Nick said, panicking as he noticed the bloody plate on the wrong side of the table.

"Really? I didn't realize you'd gotten back together. Did you, hon?"

"No, I didn't..." Sadie said, skeptically. Neither of them seemed to notice the plates.

"Oh, sure," Nick said. "We talked everything through. We're stronger than ever, honestly. She's in the bathroom," he repeated. "She should be out any second now." He looked toward the restrooms, willing her to appear.

"Well, that's great to hear," Brian said. "Look, I'm sorry I haven't been in touch lately. I was pretty steamed after what you did to her."

"Oh, sure, so was I," Nick said. "I was so ashamed. But, really, Laura and I are better than ever."

"That's amazing. I can't wait to hear all about it. So it sounds like you're doing all right then? How's the doctorate treating you?"

"Actually, I'm taking the semester off."

"Oh, sorry to hear that. Working a lot then?"

"As much as I can. Overtime, even, when I can get it. This is inside information, but I'm saving for an engagement ring."

Brian and Sadie stared at him.

"Well, good," Brian finally said.

"Yes," Sadie agreed emptily. "Our movie is starting soon. We need to go."

"All right. Let's all get together again. Real soon."

Brian nodded. "Give us a call."

The two guys embraced again while Sadie kept her distance.

"Take care, my brother," Brian said.

"Tell Laura we said hello," Sadie said sarcastically, texting furiously on her cell phone.

"I will," Nick said, waving as they walked out.

Nick leaned back in the booth and smiled widely, so wide that it could have been a frown. He switched the plates one last time and ate one last bite of steak, instantly regretting one bite too many. He signaled for the check as Carol walked by the table. When she brought it, Nick took out his credit card to pay for the meal. Laura hadn't trusted him with credit cards. She said that he lacked self-control, that he was too far in debt.

Carol came back with the receipt for him to sign.

"You know," she said, "I could see you this whole time."

Nick didn't look at her. He signed the receipt and stared at the table, frozen.

"Then you know how beautiful she is," he finally said.

Carol picked up the receipt book and tucked it under her arm. "I do," she agreed.

After she left, Nick stood to leave. The restaurant was still crowded, every booth and most of the tables. Everybody was having a good time.

"Have a good night," the hostess said as he came to the door. The rain was coming down even harder than when he'd arrived. Carol stood with the hostess. He faced them with his indeterminate smile.

"I will," he replied.

They watched him step outside. Without an umbrella, he was immediately soaked. They stood at the doorway watching him walk slowly to his car, stepping in the puddles, to go home.

THE MILKMAN

WE LOOK ALIKE, I notice right away, and I can tell by his expression that he sees it too.

"David," Jeremy says, shaking my hand. "I was so sorry to hear about your mother. I didn't hear about her passing until many months later, otherwise I certainly would've come to the funeral. She and your father meant an awful lot to me once upon a time."

That would've been a long way to go for a funeral of someone you'd lost touch with, though I suppose people do it. According to my father, my parents had hardly heard from Jeremy since he moved away more than twenty years ago.

"It's hard to believe you're an adult now," he says, taking me in from across the table. "You were the first baby I'd ever held, believe it or not. I visited you in the hospital when you were one day old. And your parents invited me over all the time. I called you 'Big D' back then. I don't suppose you remember that at all."

I was just shy of three when Jeremy moved across the country for graduate work, so, no, I don't remember. Losing him was difficult for my father. Jeremy had been his best friend, but he made so little effort to stay in touch that my father gave up trying. It hurt him. Throughout the years, my mother would occasionally say, "I miss Jeremy," when something triggered her memory, but otherwise she was unsentimental about it.

"This is going to be on one check," Jeremy says to the server when he comes to take our orders. I scan the menu for the most expensive entrées.

MY FATHER AND I had always had a good relationship. He tended to dwell on his shortcomings, but I remember him as an excellent father. He loved to read to me, and continued to do so long after I could read chapter books on my own, even re-reading me some of his favorites, like *Danny, The Champion of the World*. He was a sucker for father-son stories, and for as long as I can remember he referred to me as "my love," as Danny's father called Danny.

I was not the son he'd dreamed of having, and I felt badly about that. For instance, I never developed a passion for baseball. I played catch with him, and sometimes even initiated games of catch myself, but even as a teenager I never shook the fear of being hit in the face, and I dropped the ball a lot. He tried getting me to join a youth league, but I was never interested. He gave me relentless advice when it came to girls, but I never had a girlfriend until college, and that only served to confirm that I wasn't into girls. It bummed him out when I preferred playing video games in my room to watching a ballgame with him. But his love for me was real, and after my mother died, while I was in college, his love was even more apparent.

After graduation, I got a job close to home, and he and I were best buds again, but now without the father-son dynamics where he used to teach me about life. I'd invite myself over to watch a game with him, not because I cared about the game, but because he loved it so much, and it was amusing to watch him try to restrain his jubilation whenever I showed interest in our team. In turn, he'd go see the Marvel movies with me. And we'd get together for lunch during the work week a few times a month and just banter on.

It was during one of these lunches that he told me about Jeremy. My parents were both musicians and took as many auditions as they could as they neared graduation, but it was my mother who had gotten a job. In school, they'd been surrounded by built-in friends, peers with like interests. Now, with colleagues like Jeremy, she had built-in friends with whom to socialize, while initially my father didn't have anyone. He struggled with the transition. My mother took credit for his and Jeremy's friendship, saying that she'd worked hard on making their friendship happen.

"You know, my love," my father said. "I've long suspected that Jeremy is your biological father."

"What?!"

The way he just slipped it in there, like it couldn't have been a life-shattering statement.

"When you were born, everybody went on and on how much you looked like me. But most babies look the same and you could've looked like anyone. When you started taking shape a few years in, I kept wondering where this feature came from, where that came from. Your mother would say you had my nose, or my lips, but how many variations of lips can there be?

"I mean, look at us, David," he continued. "We look nothing alike."

He was several inches taller than me. He had somewhat darker skin from his Mediterranean heritage, while I was so light-skinned I was practically transparent. I sunburned easily, while he never did. He had a full head of dark brown hair that looked black from a distance, while I was as blond as a German and already with a receding hairline. I was asthmatic while he could run two miles without breaking a sweat.

"I never asked her about it," he said. "What good would that have done? I loved you, and I intended to keep loving you. And she and I had other problems anyway, so I kept my suspicions to myself."

I had never given any thought to the state of my parents' marriage. I saw various friends' parents split up over the years, and after the news of a split broke, we'd all talk about it at the lunch table at school, and

I'd go home and observe my own parents a little more closely. But they'd always seemed solid.

"They didn't just work together, your mother and Jeremy," my father said. "They traveled together. Sometimes it was a little day trip, going out to schools to perform for the kids, or, after school was out, at library summer programs and day camps. But sometimes there'd be an overnight, or several overnights in a row. So it wouldn't have been hard."

She was a flutist, and Jeremy played violin. The school and camp shows were part of my mother's job, along with teaching flute at the university and performing with the symphony orchestra. The performances were a half hour long and told stories of friendship and teamwork through music and motion. They even performed at my school when I was in kindergarten, she told me, and first grade as well. She'd spot me in the cluster of tiny faces and see how proud I looked that she was my mama. She said I was the most popular kid in school for a week after. Funding for the shows dried up after a few years, and her job was restructured.

"That was a fun gig," Jeremy tells me now. "I'd been doing it for a year before your mother joined. The other members came and went, but she and I held it down for four years before I left."

"Why did you leave?" I ask.

He shrugs. "It was fun, but it wasn't what I'd set out to do. I was a single guy in the Midwest, and if I wanted to do my doctorate, I figured I'd better get out before I met someone and got tied down. It was hard saying goodbye, especially to your parents. It was hard saying goodbye to you, too, to tell you the truth."

"HE HAD APPLIED to schools in secret," my father said. "And even when he went out a couple of weekends in a row for auditions in February, he didn't let on what he was doing. Not until he'd been accepted and had committed to leaving did he tell us." My father laughed. "I felt like I'd been dumped. You don't have friends like that too often. He was like a high school or college best friend, that kind of bond, but we were adults. He and I spent a weekend in Chicago together, just the two of us, saw a baseball game, went to Symphony Hall, went to the art museum where they have that Seurat, and ate ribs at a blues joint. Back home, we played softball together."

"HE CRUSHED IT to the fence," Jeremy laughs. "He was our leadoff hitter because he had the smoothest swing on the team, with a knack for hitting soft line drives in the perfect places. He must've hit .500, he was so consistent about it. And he had a reputation for bloops, too, so the outfielders played way in. And then one game out of nowhere he just pulverized the ball. Should've been a triple, easy, or even an in-side-the-parker, but the ball was back in the infield by the time he was sliding into second. He scored a couple of batters later and when he got back to the dugout he was still baffled how they'd gotten the ball in so quickly."

He pounds the table in hysterics. "'You practically touched the outfield grass rounding first base,' we told him. He didn't know how to make the turn! He was a singles hitter and had stopped at first base all sea-son, never running home to second once! That was the widest turn I'd ever seen. Probably added an extra fifty feet."

"I WAS OKAY," my father said. "I was never the best player, but I was always better than some. Jeremy was a little awkward, physically"—like me, I thought—"but he got the job done, had a little more raw power, and actually did hit a triple, once," my father said. "It was the most off-balance swing you ever saw, with a big grunt, lining it down the third base line, bouncing into the corner."

He smiled. "That was a lot of fun. It was a church team, and I'd been recruited by someone who'd also been recruited, because the church was so small that they only had six players. A few games into the season we fielded only eight guys, that was all that showed up, even with the recruits, so I recruited Jeremy. Your mother started coming to the games after that. And she started bringing you, my love."

***

JEREMY TAKES AN INHALER out of his pocket and pumps it twice.

"My allergies are always the worst this time of year," he says. "It's a good thing I don't play a wind instrument."

I don't have one on me, but I too use an inhaler, despite having played a brass instrument in high school, as had my father.

"David, it is wonderful to see you. I've thought about you more than once over the years." He smiles, and says, "Big D," while looking me over. "We'll have to stay in touch going forward." I wonder if he suspects what my father and I suspect. I'd been fantasizing about punching him in the face, flipping over the table, or jumping him in the bathroom. I had sought him out in hopes of a confession, but now that one might be imminent, I'm afraid I'll chicken out and hug him.

"And you're a grown man now! That probably doesn't seem remarkable to you, but you weren't even potty-trained the last time I saw you! You look good. I'm sorry I missed you growing up. I'll have to ask your dad to send me pictures of you from over the years."

"Why did you fall out of touch?" I ask. "If you were so close."

"We *were* close," he assures me. "I've just never been any good at long-distance relationships. I quit all social media to focus on my studies, and then it was all my career. If I'd known your mom was sick, David, I swear I would have come out to see her. And your dad."

"I'll pass that along," I say. "I'm curious to hear more about the old days, though. Tell me more about the shows you and my mother were in together."

He laughs. "Yes, those shows. Well, between the symphony, the university, and those educational shows, I spent a lot of time with your mother, more time, really, than with your father. For one show I was a donkey, and for another I was a stegosaurus. I was a farmer, once, too, and a little pig. We didn't have costumes; the kids were supposed to use their imaginations. Actually, kids are incredible at using their imaginations. They never had to ask, 'who's he supposed to be again?' By the end of the half hour, I *was* a donkey, not a man or a violinist, a donkey, and they all knew it. Your mother was a pterodactyl in one. That show was about acceptance. The three of us didn't want the other dinosaur to join our group, but by the end we recognized her value and we all became friends. And there were no words, other than when we introduced ourselves at the beginning and set up the story. We played our instruments, each with our own leitmotifs, and I hobbled around the stage like a stegosaurus would hobble, and we'd make gestures, and the kids were completely engrossed. It was an awful lot of fun, and rewarding, too."

"I wish I could remember."

"Yes, your father brought you a few times," he says.

"And this was all over the country?"

"Not really. We were advertised as a national touring group, but really we never went beyond the tri-state. Maybe they went farther after I left."

"You stayed in hotels, though, right?"

He pauses. I don't think he guesses what I'm getting at.

"Most of our shows were local. But sometimes we'd have an 8 a.m. three hours away, so we'd go up the night before. A few times there were enough shows booked that we'd stay multiple nights. That wasn't more than three or four times a year. It was fun, but we were adults. It wasn't like teenagers staying in a hotel running rampant."

"I SAID ONCE," my father said, "to your mother, 'I don't think he's my son.' Not malicious or anything. It was sort of a joke, because of how different you and I were. You were so into physics, wanting to know how everything worked, taking things apart and putting them back together. Not that you had to be into books and baseball, just because you were my son, but sometimes it was a stark contrast."

"What did mom say?"

"Oh, I don't know. Nothing really, my love. She probably whacked me on the shoulder."

He never asked her if she'd had an affair, although he suspected there might have been others even after Jeremy had moved away.

"I came home after only about an hour or two of work one morning, because I wasn't feeling well," he said. "And I saw this guy's car—someone who I already felt your mother was too close with—it wasn't parked in our driveway, or even in front of the house, it was parked on the far side of the side street, as if he didn't want to make it too obvious for the neighbors. But I saw it and recognized it anyway. And I closed my car door as softly as I could, and I entered the house as quietly as I could and glided noiselessly through the house for the bedroom."

My heart was racing.

"And?!"

"And nothing," he said. "They were in the backyard hanging laundry on the clothesline. Kind of weird, him handling our clothes like that, but it was nothing incriminating. I was almost disappointed; not that I wanted it to be true, but that I wanted to know for sure, one way or another."

"I'm relieved, at least," I said.

"When they came in, though, and saw me lying down, the guy took off, didn't even say 'hi,' even though we were supposedly friends, and your mother started talking rapidly about how all they were doing was hanging laundry. So." He shrugged. "What do you think? Should I have just asked her?"

Maybe he felt spineless for never confronting her, for being afraid of having to function without her if they split up. But I figured I was part of it, too. He probably saw that I was different from other kids, and he didn't want to make growing up any harder for me. That he'd been unhappy for so many years and hid it so well—for my benefit—I viewed as noble behavior, rather than cowardly, which made me feel a tad guilty.

"I wish you would call her 'mom,'" I said.

"What do you mean?"

"You used to call her 'mom' when you talked to me. Now you always say 'your mother.' I wish you'd go back to saying 'mom.'"

"SO YOU'RE NOT A MUSICIAN, I take it," Jeremy says now. Raised by two musicians, and possibly fathered by a third, perhaps it seems odd.

"I started on trumpet, switched to euphonium, played in band all the way through high school," I say. "I never thought I had a choice about playing, but I liked it fine and never tried to quit. It was a way to relate to my parents. But I was more into science than I ever was music. I ended up going the engineering route. I like my job."

"Were your parents okay with that, what with music being so important to them?"

"Oh, sure. They knew how hard it was to be a musician, especially my dad, who never made it full-time. They just told me to donate to arts organizations, once I made the big bucks."

"Ha! That's good. And I'm glad they were supportive. You probably make more money than I do. What do you do exactly?"

"I design components and systems for laboratory automation." He looks at me blankly, not unlike the way my father looks when I talk about my job. "Basically, I develop machines that automate repetitive manual tasks in lab settings for better accuracy and precision."

He laughs. "Wow! I don't even know what that means, but that's fantastic! Big D using the big words. You're an impressive young man. And here I am thinking highly of myself for playing Beethoven. Good for you."

"Beethoven is nothing to sneeze at," I say.

"No, he's not," he laughs again. "This is nice. How about your dad? Does he still play much?"

"Hardly at all," I say. "Maybe in church at Christmas and Easter."

"That's too bad," Jeremy says. "He was a good French horn player. He'd sub with the symphony, and he gigged around town. It's a shame he could never make a full-time living through music. I always thought he had the talent, and he sure had the drive, but I think his anxiety got in the way, or maybe he just had bad breaks. He'd make self-deprecating comments about 'playing second fiddle' to your mother, and it annoyed him how often people introduced him as 'his wife is the principal flutist of the symphony.' I admired him for working as hard at it as he did. Like I said, he was good enough; I really believed that. I'm sorry to hear he gave up."

"He has a lot of regrets about it."

"I thought he was good enough," Jeremy repeats. "What a shame. Do you think he'll get married again? Has he been dating?"

"He's been on a few dates," I say. "But I really don't know if he'll get married again. He doesn't act that interested."

"And what about you? I don't see a ring."

"No ring," I say. "You either, I see."

"No, I've never been married. At this point, I expect to be a lifelong bachelor." He shrugs. "Do you at least have a girlfriend?"

"No, no girlfriend," I say. "No boyfriend, either."

"Boyfriend!" he says, and laughs. When I don't laugh, he says, "seriously?"

I nod. He frowns.

MY FATHER HAD BEEN an absolute wreck during my mother's final days. We assumed the treatments would keep her alive for decades, like with so many others. But it kept spreading, and only five months after her initial diagnosis, she was gone. My father and I cried together in her hospital room every time she fell asleep, afraid this was the time she wouldn't wake up again.

"You still loved her," I said.

He nodded.

"But do you regret not asking her? Did you consider asking her at the end?"

He shook his head. "I didn't think about it every day. I didn't think about it at all the entire time she was sick. She wasn't a bad woman. And she was a great mother to you. That's what was important."

By the time the funeral was over and the crowds had dispersed, it was spring break. I suggested to my father that we go down to Florida for spring training, something he'd long wanted to do, but he said he wasn't up for it. I hung around, anyway, to look after him and keep him company.

That was the week I came out to him. I hadn't planned it but the timing seemed right. He said he wasn't surprised. Always an affectionate father, he gave me a big hug and kiss. For a few years, as a teenager, I pretended that his affection embarrassed me, but by college I'd embraced it again. He was my best friend, it had occurred to me, and always had been.

But otherwise he didn't know how to talk about it. He recommended books with gay or bi characters, and I read *The Mysteries of Pittsburgh* and *Giovanni's Room*. He'd recommend bands like Against Me! because "Their singer is openly trans." He'd ask if I was seeing anyone, or if I had my eye on anyone. I wouldn't say it necessarily brought us closer together, but it didn't drive us apart either.

For weeks after he first told me his suspicions about my mother, I pressed him for more information; he'd been nonchalant about it at first, but seemed borderline annoyed when I continued questioning him about it. He said it shouldn't change the way I remembered her, that she loved me to pieces. And I didn't view her as any less of a mother. But I was obsessed that she had apparently failed him as a wife.

But what that meant, I didn't know. I would never have a wife, nor did I think I knew just what a wife needed to be. I searched the nether regions of my memory for instances of affection between them. I remembered one kiss, maybe when I was in middle school, after which my father joked, "I'd like more of that," at which my mother rolled her eyes, so maybe it wasn't the joke he pretended it to be. In the hospital, he kissed her forehead a lot. But beyond that, I don't remember much at all: kissing, hugging, saying "I love you," not much. I'd never had a problem with the knowledge that my parents had had sex at least once to have me, or that they'd probably continued to have sex, though I never dwelt on the details. But now I wondered if they hadn't done it as often as I'd assumed.

My father speculated that she'd given up on him after it was apparent that he wouldn't catch up with her, professionally. He and his French horn had repeatedly failed to crack that next tier, and she must have gotten tired of dragging him along. And maybe she had passively encouraged him to give up on his dream, like shooting a horse with a broken leg, but then when he did give up she didn't respect the unartistic desk job he'd resorted to, either.

It was shocking to think of the undertones I'd missed throughout my childhood and adolescence. My best memories had been of the three of us simply being a family at home.

I had made up my mind that I was going to track Jeremy down and see if I could find anything out from him. I knew he was a violin professor, and, once I got his last name, it wasn't hard to find his faculty profile on his university's website. We looked alike. Seeing his head shot on the website, I was disheartened to see his blond hair and pale complexion. I concocted a simple lie in an e-mail—"I'm going to be in Greensboro two weeks from now, and my father suggested I look you up. I understand you were close with my parents many years ago"—to which he replied that he would love to meet me and would gladly treat me to a fine meal.

"I have no proof whatsoever," my father tried to impress upon me. "It's important to remember that. I could very well be wrong about everything."

So I didn't tell my father I was doing this. With any luck, he wouldn't even know I'd gone.

"LISTEN," I SAY, psyching myself up to the main event. "I have an ulterior motive for seeking you out. My father didn't really suggest it; I found you on my own."

"Oh?"

"Well, he and I have been talking a lot about my mother and their marriage. And, well."

I'm so nervous I'm shaking. But I've come this far, so I finally ask:

"Are you my real father?"

Jeremy doesn't say anything, and freezes. I'm prepared to expound on my father's suspicions, but my question ought to stand for itself. Finally he moves and clears his throat.

"I suppose your father thinks so, and that's why you have the idea."

I still don't say anything. He owes me an explanation, I feel, and I don't want to get in the way of that, although if I was going to get violent, this would be the moment.

"He and I used to be great friends," he says. "For about four years he was one of the best friends I ever had. But I left solely for my career, and whether or not I loved your mother had nothing to do with it."

He looks at me, just as he had when we first sat down. The resemblance is there; anybody passing by would think we were related.

"So you'll need to get that idea out of your head. I don't have a son, and I'm not your father. I knew you when you were first born, and that's it. All right?"

He signals for the check and our server brings it momentarily. I think he's a prick, but tears form in my eyes anyway. He ignores my tears, nor does he say anything else as he pays the check and gathers himself to leave.

"Nice to see you again, David," he says once we're outside the restaurant. "Take care of your father."

He doesn't say anything about staying in touch or getting to know each other better, as he had earlier.

He offers a handshake before turning to walk down the street. I think I know everything I need to know. At least I don't want to know anything else.

I decide to call my father and tell him what I've done.

"Hello, my love," he says, when he answers the phone.

No Amends

WITH MY BEST POKER FACE, I accept Neil's offer of a Bud Light to show that a) I'm not disgusted by cheap beer and b) I don't look down on him for having poor taste. I *am* disgusted, though, and I *do* look down on him. I'm a find-a-microbrew-I've never tried-before kind of guy. It seems Neil is still a loser.

He was *always* a gigantic loser. Everybody thought so, not just me. He was a natural target, and I was far from the only guy who was an asshole to him. But I was perhaps his biggest tormentor. I remember when I was twenty or twenty-one, home from college for the summer, I had plans to attend a bonfire with my best friends from middle and high school. I got a call from the hostess warning me that Neil had been invited, certainly not by her, and she was worried how I would react.

How *would* I have reacted? Frankly, with shame. I hadn't seen Neil since high school. But beyond the embarrassment I felt for having treated him like dogs-hit for so many years, I truly didn't have a problem with him.

So I attended the bonfire, despite the warning, and fantasized that maybe Neil and I could step off to the side for a moment or two and I could apologize for being a dick to him, hoping that he wouldn't ask me why I had been a dick, since there truly hadn't ever been a real reason. But he didn't come. I think my friend, the hostess, somehow found a way to keep him from coming. Maybe she told him it had been cancelled, lying to him to protect me.

I open and sip my Bud Light and I imagine that this is what piss must taste like. My inclination is to chug it down and get it over with, but what would I do if, seeing it empty, he offered me a second Bud Light?

I've been in this house before. It's Neil's parents' house, or it had been. They have retired to Florida and Neil has moved in. Neil and I are the same age and grew up on the same street, and I have distant memories of playdates our parents set up back in kindergarten, first, or second grade. Even with the naiveté of a six-year-old I remember thinking that the house was trashy. Even now it has a stale musty smell. The decades-old linoleum may have been white when it was new but it's a dirty mustard now.

Somewhere I must have decided that if I didn't want to be at the bottom of the social totem pole, I'd have to make sure somebody else was instead. We made fun of the fact that his father was a garbageman and that his mother worked at Wal-Mart; the rest of us had parents with staunchly white-collar jobs. And in the mornings, we chucked snowballs at him as we waited for the school bus. He was an easy target, by which I mean he was a big target. That's another thing that didn't make sense. He could have easily kicked my ass and probably most of our classmates' asses. But he didn't. I don't remember him in a single fight. I don't remember him ever defending himself.

"Let's sit down," he suggests. We've been standing in the kitchen on the antiquated linoleum around the same kitchen island I remember sitting around as a small child while his mother sang songs and told jokes in the hope that her son's would-be friend would have a good time.

I'm wary of sitting down. I'm wary of being here, in general, not because he is a loser and I don't want to be seen with him—one of the perks of being an adult is not caring about being cool—but because if I were him, I would want revenge. If I were him, I would have dreamed for years of how to lure myself into his basement torture chamber where I would, over the next several weeks, gradually scrape off pieces of my skin while recounting all the ways I'd wronged myself.

When he and I had run into each other this morning, I had suggested we grab a drink, and I'd meant at a bar, but instead we are here.

"It's good to see you," he says as he ushers me into the living room. "I almost didn't recognize you at first. Not in a bad way. You've aged a lot better than some of us. Better than I have," he adds with a laugh. "But you still look a little different."

I'd recognized him in the grocery store because he looks almost exactly the same, except a) a bit fatter, and b) with a bad comb-over covering a bald spot instead of the full head of scraggly greasy hair he'd sported during our formative years.

"I'm sixty pounds heavier than I was at graduation," I allow.

"You were a twig."

I *had* been a twig, and he'd been at least sixty pounds heavier than I was, as well as a few inches. He could have played football. I've never thought about that before. Why hadn't he? I wonder how different his life would have been if he had. Maybe he would have been good and the other football players would have convinced him to do his hair differently and to throw his Looney Tunes shirts into the garbage.

"You're doing really well," he continues, and I assume he doesn't mean my appearance, which isn't bad for a forty-year-old but is certainly nothing to brag about. "You seem like you keep pretty busy, and your kids look great. You have a nice-looking family."

He must have been on my Facebook profile. We're not friends on Facebook, although there have been times that he and I have commented on the same mutual acquaintance's post. Twice by my recollection, upon seeing my comments he typed, "Joel, good to see you!" to which I'd reply, "Neil, how are you!" But I never sent him a friend request after any of those brief and shallow interactions, nor did he ever send me one.

"Appreciate that," I say, instead of accusing him of being a Facebook stalker. I'm not really doing that well but I'm involved in a lot of projects so it looks like I am. In fact, my wife makes more money than I do, although she doesn't really make that much either. Of the kids, I add, "They keep me busy." Then I say, "You ever been married?" For a second I cringe at my intrusiveness, but I still want to know.

He doesn't seem to mind, though, and shakes his head. "I've had girlfriends," he says, which I hope is true but doubt, "but I've never actually considered marrying any of them." He laughs as if nobody has quite been good enough for him.

But yeah right. Girlfriends? Ha! More like yellow page escorts, Lyell Avenue prostitutes, and mail-order Russian brides who bolt the second he picks them up at the airport.

There I go again with my natural tendency to bully him. And the irony is of course that I wasn't popular in high school either. I had friends, yes, and occasional girlfriends, both of which set me apart from him, but I also got bullied. This one dude, Rob, was the biggest prick to me, although when I complained, my mother excused him by saying he was having trouble dealing with his parents' divorce. Yet the bullies like Rob who made me feel two feet tall I rarely give any thought to anymore, while over the years I have frequently regretted being a dick to Neil.

Neil looks at me curiously as I sit in the only non-cushioned chair in the room before he sits down in a recliner. I've selected this wooden chair because a) I want to be able to jump up the moment I feel an attack coming, and a deep cushion might slow me down, and b) everything looks like it's been here since our kindergarten playdates thirty-five years ago and I don't want to sit in anything cushioned that has been collecting sweat, dust mites, and dead skin cells for all these decades. He reclines back and lifts the footrest and I realize that if there's going to be an attack it won't be from him but from someone I can't see, someone I don't even realize is here, who's going to sneak up behind me, or maybe wait until I need to use the bathroom, another reason not to finish the Bud Light.

"What's your brother up to these days," I ask, remembering Hunter who, it occurs to me, might be lurking and ready to attack at Neil's signal. "And your sister," I add, suddenly remembering he had one of those, too, whatever her name was. Though both younger, to my recollection neither the brother or sister were pariahs the way Neil had been. Hunter was actually kind of cool, I think, and played drums in a rock band.

"Allison is good," he says. "She works in insurance. She's married and has three daughters," he chuckles. "Yikes, right? That's a lot of girls. Anyway, they live in Columbus."

"Ohio?" I ask, and he nods. That's six hours away. "Uncle Neil," I say. "And Hunter?"

He laughs again, this time heavier and forced. "I don't even know! Sometimes Allison updates me about him, but I never see Hunter. He lives in Los Angeles." He shrugs. "Still playing drums."

"That's good," I say. Being a musician in LA seems like it would be a cool life. "I'm sorry you're not in touch, though."

"Yeah, the last time I heard from him was because he thinks it's bullshit that I'm living here. He was saying the house should belongs equally to the three of us and that if I live here I need to pay him and Allison their shares of what the house is worth."

"Oh," I say, uncomfortable.

"But then my parents stepped in and told him to knock it off because they still own the house and they're not dead yet so no one's paying anyone anything. But, you want to know a secret?" He smirks as he looks at me conspiratorially. "They're leaving me the house in their will."

"Good for you!"

He nods in satisfaction. "Allison knows, and she's okay with it, and she says she won't tell Hunter." He shrugs. "It doesn't really matter, anyway. They're not going to die for another ten or fifteen years."

He lets down the foot of his recliner and stands up. "Do you want another beer?" he asks, shaking his empty can.

"I'm still nursing this one," I say, gesturing to my Bud Light, which is three-quarters full.

He walks toward the kitchen and I stand up to turn around and make sure nobody can sneak up on me.

I spy the top of a Playboy on an end table. I lean over to uncover it a tad more and see that it's a) a recent edition and b) addressed to Neil; he's a subscriber.

And then I remember seeing Playboy at this house before. His dad had been a subscriber, and there had been an issue lying around when I'd been over. Neil's mother had scooped the magazine up, lightly commenting that her husband shouldn't leave that kind of thing lying around.

But I wouldn't have known what Playboy was when I was in kindergarten or first grade. So this memory must be from when I was ten or eleven, at least. What was I doing here then? Didn't I hate him by this point? By age eleven, wasn't I already throwing snowballs at his broad backside?

Neil comes back with a fresh can of Bud Light and pops it open before sinking back into his recliner.

Age ten or eleven would have been fifth grade. Fifth grade had been a bad year for me, the first school year after my parents had split up over the summer. I'd been in therapy, and I had anger issues for the next several years until roughly junior year of high school. Neil was not in my fifth grade class, or fourth either, I'm pretty sure. And sixth grade is when we started changing classes for every subject, and I was in all accelerated courses, while Neil was not, so I rarely saw him except for the bus stop. What the hell could I have been doing here at an age old enough to know what Playboy was?

"You look funny," he says.

"I just had a flashback of being here in like fifth grade," I admit. "Just trying to remember the circumstances."

"I remember," he says. "I remember trying to show you this project I was working on in the basement, some electrical switchboard I had in mind that was going to control the lights in the entire neighborhood. I wanted to be Lex Luthor," he giggles. "But I couldn't even get it to turn on and off the lights in the basement. And you were so bored. I remember kicking myself later, after you left, as if I'd blown my chance. Like, 'you idiot, Joel finally came over, and you bored the pants off of him.'"

A messy basement of wiring and solder smell vaguely comes back to me. "But what was I doing here?" I feel ashamed for wording it this way, as if there had to have been a reason other than just wanting to play with a neighborhood boy.

But Neil isn't bothered. For decades he's been resigned to the idea that no one would spend time with him if he didn't have to.

"Your dad was moving out," he says. "So your mom arranged for you to be here all day. I was under strict instructions not to let you look out the front windows where you might see the moving van. My mother was on guard, too. You wanted to watch a movie, but the TV was in the front room"—here he gestures to the current television, somewhat newer but in the same place his childhood television had been years ago—"so we stayed in the basement most of the time."

One day, my dad's stuff was gone. I had never wondered before about the logistics of his moving out. I guess subconsciously I assumed he'd carried boxes out of the house during the middle of the night, while I was asleep. My parents sat me down one day to tell me they were splitting up, after which my father left. Then I kept noticing that certain things had disappeared.

"So you knew my parents were splitting up before I knew," I say, bitterly. I don't give my parents' divorce much thought anymore, it's been so long, but of all the kids my age to learn about it before me, why did it have to be Neil? Surely they could have found somebody else to take me for the day.

He shrugs. "We didn't know if you knew or not," he says. "I was told not to bring it up."

I stew on it for a minute. Then I change the subject and go into attack mode.

"So Allison married in Columbus, Hunter gigging in California, and your parents retired in Florida," I say, and maliciously add, "and you're here all alone."

"Sure, I wish they were all closer," he says, my intent going over his head. "But I'm not lonely. I have a date coming over later, actually."

A date, ha! A hooker. I knew it! Men who subscribe to Playboy need to pay for sex. I look around the room and think about all the prostitutes who've been right here in the house where I had apparently come over to play a couple of times as a child.

I smirk, taking satisfaction from his pathetic-ness, still annoyed about his role in distracting me from my father moving out.

"Yeah? What's her name?" I ask.

I think to myself that if he says Vixen, or Krystal, or Candi-with-an-i that I'm going to stand up and walk out of here without giving an explanation.

"Her name's Cheryl."

"Cheryl," I repeat. That doesn't sound like a hooker name.

"Yeah, you know her."

"I do?"

"You took her to prom," he says. "Cheryl Holland."

"Oh!" I say. Cheryl had been a genuinely hot underclassmen who hadn't been one of my girl-friends but *had* been a fun prom date. "I'm surprised you remember."

"We both remember," he says, and I'm about to joke that "Cheryl sure had better remember!" when he adds, "we were both there."

"You went to prom?" I say. And there it is again, my jerk-off implication that he was too much of a loser to go to prom.

"Of course I went to prom," he says.

I want to ask who his date was, but I restrain myself. At the moment, I'm over my annoyance about my day at his house and I'm back to pity. I don't want to hear him admit that he went to the prom stag.

"It would be fun to see Cheryl again," I say. I haven't seen her since high school, either, though she and I are friends on Facebook. I'm not about to say this out loud, but she's aged terribly, much worse than Neil or I have.

"Well," he says, suddenly serious. "No offense, but I'd rather you didn't, to be honest."

"What? Why?"

"I like Cheryl. But if she sees you she might not be interested in me anymore."

"But I'm married."

He shrugs. "Still. This is our third date, but it's her first time coming over. That's why it's so picked up in here."

Other than the Playboy, I acknowledge that the house is clutter-free, even though it is still kind of dingy and smelly. But I tell him that I won't see Cheryl, although I think to myself that maybe I'll reach out to her anyway, even if it's just a private message that says, "hope you had fun with Neil, ha ha ha ha."

And with that natural impulse I let go of the fantasy I've had for most of my adulthood and acknowledge to myself that, no matter what, I'll never be friends with Neil.

"Neil," I begin, deciding to get to it. "I don't think of myself as an asshole, but I've always been an asshole to you, and I don't know why."

"I know," he says. He doesn't seem surprised that I'm bringing it up. I'm annoyed that he's agreeing with me so amiably. "I don't think of you as an asshole, either," he says.

I'm reminded of the time my father dragged me down the street to Neil's doorstep and forced me to apologize to him face-to-face after a particular assault that day in school had been serious enough to warrant a call home from the principal. "He's not Ferris Bueller," my father had lectured to me, "and he knows he's not Ferris Bueller. Not everyone can be Ferris Bueller. But it doesn't mean you can't treat him like Ferris Bueller."

And there I stood outside of his door, in front of this kid who was nearly twice my size, who hadn't fought back when I'd punched him a bunch of times in the arm—unfortunately within sight of a teacher. I couldn't even make eye contact with him because I knew my dad was right, and I knew I was wrong, and I knew Neil didn't deserve it; he sure as hell hadn't done anything to provoke me; he hadn't done anything but exist. He was and is.

"I don't have a reason," I say.

"There was no reason," he says. He's very calm, not as if he expected that I would want to make amends, but as if he would have been okay with whatever direction the afternoon took.

"I don't know why we couldn't have been friends," I say.

"No reason that I ever figured out," he says.

I'm dangerously close to crying and I fight to swallow the frog in my throat. I don't want to give him the satisfaction of blubbering in his living room.

"I wish you would've fought back," I say. "Even now, part of me wishes you would punch me."

He stands and I jump up to defend myself, but he doesn't notice as he walks to the kitchen. "Want another beer?"

I say no, and reach down to take a swig of my still half-full Bud Light, now approaching room temperature.

When he returns, I ask, "Why don't you hit me?"

But he sits back in his recliner and pops open his beer.

"If I wanted to hit you I would've hit you years ago. But you...some people are like that. You and I had some sort of disconnect, like my damn switchboard, you know? It looked good on paper, but it just wasn't going to work. I don't lose sleep over it. I really am glad you're doing so well."

"I'm glad you're doing well, too," I say, and this time my voice cracks and I can't suppress the frog in my throat. "And I'm sorry."

I stand up. "I think I should go."

He doesn't object, and stands up too. At the door, I ask him, "who was your date to the prom?"

"Allison," he replies.

I'm not facing him so he can't see my wide eyes and look of disgust. But from behind, my body language must have given it away, and he laughs.

"It's a joke. I wouldn't've actually taken my sister."

Yet for a second it seemed entirely possible that a loser like him would have taken his younger sister to the prom. I curse myself for so easily believing it.

"No one's ever had a lower opinion of me than you," he says, laughing again.

I turn to face him, and he sticks out his hand to shake. Part of me doesn't want to touch him, but the other part wants to throw my arms around him and give him a bear hug. I shake his hand, firmly, and for perhaps a second longer than I normally would.

As I walk to my car, I look in the direction of my childhood home, where neither of my parents live anymore. You can see it, a little, but not as well as thirty years ago; some of the trees between here and there have filled out. What confusing horror it would have been for me, at the age of eleven, to look out Neil's front window to see a moving van in front of my house. My resentment dissipates and I appreciate the effort Neil and his mother made that day to keep me from finding out prematurely.

I turn around and look at him. For a second, it looks like there's a shadow of a second person lingering inside behind Neil. But I can't tell for sure.

"Tell Cheryl hello for me," I call from the driveway.

"I'm not going to," he says, and he laughs, and I laugh, too.

TWENTY YEARS OF FUTILITY

- 1 -

FOURTH GRADE is almost over. Today, Ms. Dibble gave out awards. These awards aren't really for achievements so much as for defining personal identities. Mike won "Class Runner" because he likes to run even though he's not the fastest—last week Scott raced him at recess and won! Andrea got "Class Calm" because nobody's ever heard her speak. Shane got "Class Hair" because he uses hairspray. Ms. Dibble crowned me "Class Pirates Fan." It's not really a compliment. This is Rochester, New York, and I'm the only Pirates fan anybody knows.

In a letter I beg Barry Bonds not to leave the team. My father addresses it to Three Rivers Stadium and sticks it in the mailbox. But Bonds signs a record-setting contract with the Giants; my father tells me during church. I hear there was no chance Bonds was going to re-sign with them. I guess the Pirates didn't even make an offer.

I'm nine-years-old. The Pirates won't see another winning season for a very long time.

- 2 -

WITH A BASEBALL BAT in hand, I'm wearing a Pirates helmet, a Pirates shirt, my Little League pants, and cleats. It's Halloween and I'm Pirates center fielder Andy Van Slyke! As I go door to door in Rochester, no one gets it. It doesn't help that, without Bonds and Bonilla protecting him in the lineup, Van Slyke has stopped hitting.

Drabek has left, too, and Van Slyke isn't far behind. This is the Pirates' first of what will become four consecutive five-year rebuilding plans. My favorite players are gone. Maybe I can find hope in the farm system.

Dad and I drive to Buffalo to see the Pirates' triple-A team. It's Midre Cummings poster night! I hang mine on my wall. The Pirates and the Bisons both bill Cummings as the next Barry Bonds. He doesn't live up to the hype. Now we have Kris Benson, the first overall pick in the draft. But why doesn't he pitch better? He finishes his career better known for his wife—a former stripper and murder suspect—than for his actual baseball accomplishments.

All of my friends like baseball. Matt likes the Blue Jays. Kevin likes the Orioles. Tim likes the Mets. Liking the Yankees are Steve, Mark, Jon, Tony, Chris, Greg, and pretty much everyone else I know. The Yankees are building a dynasty. My friends have shameless man-crushes on Andy Pettitte, rookie Derek Jeter, and even Scott Brosius. At the lunch table they call Paul O'Neill "Paulie" and Tino Martinez "Constantino". I'm jealous but I roll my eyes and keep my mouth shut.

- 3 -

MY NEW FAVORITE PLAYER—Outside Candidates:

1.   Kirby Puckett. The Puck has a fun name and he's always smiling on his baseball cards. I work in my neighbor's garden for an entire week to save up enough money to buy his 1985 Topps Rookie Card. For years I've had a plaque hanging on my wall commemorating his career. But he goes blind during spring training, with so many of my impressionable years remaining.

2.   Ken Griffey Jr. Junior is the best player in baseball, and who better to root for than the best? I even have a Griffey Jr. #24 shirt and a poster of him on my wall; Sears didn't have any Pirates shirts. But the Mariners play on the West Coast, and the newspapers rarely have their box scores.

3.   Cal Ripken Jr. The Iron Man is a good citizen and he even played a season in Rochester before getting called up to Baltimore. I hear old guys romanticize Ripken's brief stop in Rochester: "He was a sure thing, all right, if there ever was one. He was only here about

a year, but everyone could tell, just take one look at him. Even when he fielded a routine grounder, or hit a routine fly ball, you could just sense it. It was a big league fly ball. He was destined for greatness, and it was obvious." But Ripken is becoming a national hero and while I wish him no ill will, there's nothing special about rooting for the same guy as the rest of the country.

Puckett, Griffey, and Ripken all play in the American League, you note. I can't bear the thought of my new favorite player facing the Pirates.

- 4 -

"WHY DO YOU LIKE the Pirates?"

They ask out of honest curiosity, as if everyone in New York State should root for either the Mets or the Yankees, never mind that it's a shorter drive from Rochester to Pittsburgh, Cleveland, Toronto, or even (slightly) to Boston, than it is to New York City.

"My dad grew up in Pennsylvania and rooted for the Pirates and Steelers, so I do too."

"Do you also like the Penguins?"

"I don't follow hockey."

Or:

"The Pirates suck so much. Oh my God, they're terrible. Not one guy on your team would make the Yankees roster."

Yes, they suck, and yes, they're terrible, but, for the record, just this past year the Pirates traded Charlie Hayes to the Yankees who later caught the final out of the 1996 World Series, so not true.

- 5 -

WHAT IF THE PIRATES LEAVE Pittsburgh? That's all anyone's talking about. Will I continue rooting for them? I don't know! Having never lived there, my tie to the city of Pittsburgh is the baseball team, not the other way around. I only like them because my father likes them. It's his fault. I didn't choose this team—I inherited them.

Grandpa didn't follow sports. Dad grew up in Pennsylvania but back in the sixties the Steelers were and always had been terrible and most of his friends rooted for out-of-town teams. Grandma and Grandpa *used* to live in Pittsburgh, though. They lived on top of Mt. Washington, which overlooks the three rivers. I guess that's why Dad went with Pittsburgh teams. The Pirates may blow, but at least I'm not a Browns fan.

***

- 6 -

MY YANKEES FAN FRIENDS are mostly Buffalo Bills fans, too. This helps a little. The similarities between the Pirates and Bills are a little jarring. The Pirates lost the NLCS three years in a row from 1990-1992, while the Bills lost the Super Bowl *four* years in a row from 1990-1993 (B-I-L-L-S: **B**oy **I** **L**ove **L**osing **S**uper Bowls—Ha!). The heartbreak that Bills fans felt following the fourth Super Bowl loss was probably more painful, but Pirates fans have a strong case. As the 1992 baseball season was coming to a close, Pirates fans were fairly certain that, regardless of how the postseason played out,   they were due for a down period—there was no "wait 'til next year" mantra to fall back on—though no one imagined twenty years of futility. After the fourth Super Bowl loss, though, Jim Kelly stuck around and Bills fans still had reason to believe they could remain competitive.

- 7 -

ON A CLEAR NIGHT we can pick up KDKA 1020 Pittsburgh on the car radio. It's not crystal clear, but still, that's Lanny Frattare's play-by-play announcing! Dad swerves all over the road to avoid power lines that interfere with the signal. Denny Neagle is in a bases loaded two-out jam. *Static.* What's going on?! Dad drifts to the right and then all the way into the next lane. I stare intensely at the car stereo hoping that I've developed a super power that will clear the signal up. Neither works. Dad drifts to the left. The nearest on-coming car is up a ways. He drifts further and we're driving on the wrong side of the road! I'm not worried. Well, I am, but not about crashing; I'm worried about the game! Finally the power line juts away and we get the signal back. Commercials. What happened?! Did he get out of it? Did he strike him out? Is this a pitching change? Did they score? Did the opposing batter hit a bases clearing double but was then thrown out trying to stretch it into a triple? We will find out after the break, but only if we stay away from those damn power lines.

This stop sign has always been a good place to pick up the distant radio station. If the game is especially intense we pull over at this intersection for ten or fif-teen minutes and shoo anyone who pulls up behind us around. Our driveway is a total dead zone. After pull-ing in we race inside the house where whoever gets there first dials up the modem and, after only a couple of minutes and a failed connection or three, a world of information is at our fingertips. To me, a world of information is good for one thing: baseball scores. I stay glued to the computer screen, hitting refresh ev-ery thirty seconds to follow the count: 1 ball 0 strikes; 1 ball 1 strike; 1 ball 2 strikes (foul); 2 balls 2 strikes; ball in play; groundout shortstop to first base; 1 out.

***

- 8 -

J.D. HAS LIVED IN ROCHESTER all of his life but his father is a Pittsburgh native so J.D. inherited the Pirates, too. Against all odds, I've gone from not knowing ANY Pirates fans to knowing several, now that J.D. and his family have moved in only five houses away.

Together J.D. and I idolize Jason Kendall, get excited when we pull a Kevin Young baseball card out of a pack, and argue over who gets to draft Al Martin—a breakout player any year now—in fantasy baseball. We play Hardball 5 on his CD-Rom, beefing up the Pirates players' skill levels which turn Kevin Polcovich into a .340 hitter and Francisco Cordova into a Cy Young contender. We force the computer to trade us Ken Griffey Jr. and Randy Johnson. The Hardball 5 Pirates are on pace to win 140 games, the greatest team the world has ever seen!

All offseason long J.D. and I write out the Pirates projected 25-man roster. Next to their names, we predict their stats. Everyone is due for improvement. On paper, we see no reason why the Pirates won't contend next year. Sports Illustrated doesn't agree with us, which we don't understand.

A Frisbee, a Tupperware lid, and an old Rochester Red Wings hat are first, second, and third base. Home plate is that area where the grass is worn away. We only need four people to get a game going. In J.D.'s backyard, he and I are the Pirates, he in the outfield with me pitching. There's no umpire and because calling balls and strikes leads to more arguments than anything else, it's only a strike if you swing; there are no walks. Ryan on the Yankees is taking advantage of the rule. He's sitting on everything! Waiting for a nice fat one down the middle of the plate to hammer! This wouldn't bother me so much if I had better control but my accuracy is garbage. I'm just chucking it in there, hoping it'll be close enough to entice a swing. I've thrown twenty pitches this at bat. I'm sure Ryan would've struck out at least twice if we had an umpire. I'm pissed. I drill him in the back.

Ryan charges the mound and punches me in the nose. The punch isn't powerful so much as unexpected. I check to see if my nose is bleeding—it's not—and I lunge at him, tackle him, and wail away, too nervous to punch him in the face but pounding him in the chest and the sides, where he's wearing a sweatshirt and it probably doesn't even hurt. J.D. eventually pulls me off.

Another day, J.D. says he's figured out how to throw a forkball. I'm not positive what a forkball is supposed to do, but I crush the first one he throws, a mammoth shot that crashes into the neighbor's shutter. The neighbor complains to J.D.'s parents. J.D. is grounded and I go home crying.

***

- 9 -

NOBODY ELSE IS AROUND and J.D. and I grow restless. Hardball 5 isn't cutting it at the moment, and we've already looked at our baseball cards a million times. The newspaper says the Pirates are playing at this very moment! Jon Leiber is starting for the Bucs and we're dying to know how he's doing.

There's internet at my father's house, the only Internet we know of. It's almost a ten-minute drive to get there, and we figure it will take twenty on bikes. We take off, stopping to buy sodas, and dropping our sodas in the street when we're almost run over by a car. Forty-five minutes later we arrive.

Dad's not home and I don't have a key. The backdoor to the garage is unlocked. Once inside, we set up the ladder so I can reach the spare key. We're in! We make a beeline to the computer where I sign into AOL. We each take turns going to the bathroom since it will be several minutes before the dial-up connection is complete.

We hear footsteps in another part of the house. We step away from the computer to investigate. Around the corner come two big men in uniform. My neighbor called to report two boys breaking into a house, we're told.   I'm only thirteen and I don't have a driver's license or any other way to prove that I have every right to be here. It takes some explaining and searching but finally I find a framed picture of me that seems to clear things up for the cops.

My mother and J.D.'s father are summoned to pick us up. Everyone is pretty upset and J.D. will probably get grounded again. I don't see the big deal. It's true we didn't tell anyone where we were going, but how can I "break in" to my own house? It's not my fault the idiot neighbor doesn't know who I am. I sneak away to finally check the Pirates score before we have to go. They're losing.

- 10 -

PART OF THE PROBLEM with rooting for the Pirates is I don't know what any of them look like. The players on Hardball 5 aren't distinguishable other than skin color and right- or left-handedness. To watch live baseball my best option is the Saturday Game of the Week, but the Pirates are never on the Game of the Week. For their actual faces, unless I happen to be at a friend's house and catch the Pirates playing the Cubs, Braves, or Mets on cable, I have to depend on baseball cards.

The baseball card industry has taken a hit following the players' strike. For some reason, Topps has reduced the size of its base sets. The 1996 set has only 440 cards, down from 825 in 1993. Because the sets are smaller there isn't room for the "lesser" players, your middle relievers, bench players, most Pirates. Dave Wainhouse doesn't get a card. If I want to know what Dave Wainhouse looks like, I have to go to Pittsburgh and buy a yearbook at Three Rivers Stadium.

Aside from birthdays and Christmas, few things are more exciting than opening the first baseball cards of the new season. Okay, here's my first pack: Hank Aaron reprint, cool; Tony Gwynn, nice; no Pirates though. What a gyp. Second pack: I see a Pirate! Who the hell is Warren Morris? A rookie, I guess. Third pack: Jason Kendall! Yes! I will take this to school tomorrow to show my friends but no one will care.

- 11 -

I WATCH THE ALL-STAR GAME to the very end in hopes of catching a glimpse of the lone obligatory Pirates representative enter the game in the eighth inning as a defensive replacement. He'll inevitably get left on deck when the final out of the game is made. When Turner Ward makes a running catch in San Diego and knocks down the outfield wall after crashing into it, I set up the VCR to record the "top plays of the week" segment on the local news station and eventually wear out the VHS tape watching it over and over. Francisco Cordova and Ricardo Rincon combine for a ten-inning no-hitter, the Pirates winning it on a three-run home run by former Rochester Red Wing Mark Smith—big picture of him in the local paper afterwards—and I hang the article in my room for years.

Rincon gets traded to the Indians for Brian Giles, and I'm sorry to see him go, even if Giles instantly becomes our best player. But I'm filled with pride when Rincon becomes the subject of my favorite chapter of *Moneyball*, and later the subject of my favorite scene in the movie.

- 12 -

PNC PARK IS BUILT and essentially saves baseball in Pittsburgh. Dad and I journey to the stadium a couple of weeks into its inaugural season but it's snowing and the game is officially postponed before we're halfway there. We finish the trip anyway, take in the stadium's exterior, and check out the monuments—new Willie Stargell statue!—before turning around to head back to Rochester.

PNC Park is the toast of Major League Baseball, losing points only for its team's quality of play. The Onion publishes "PNC Park Threatens To Leave Pittsburgh Unless Better Team Is Built."

J.D., Kris, and I go to Pittsburgh for a game. Brennan and his girlfriend happen to be in Pittsburgh, too, looking for an apartment. A Monday night game. J.D., Kris, and I have seats in the upper deck. Minutes later Brennan and his girlfriend sit down at the other end of our row. That we bought tickets next to each other is a tremendous coincidence considering the tens of thousands of empty seats to choose from in PNC Park that night. It's the fourth inning, and, Hey! Brian Meadows hasn't allowed a hit yet! I say this out loud and everyone gets kind of pissed at me for jinxing it. Meadows almost immediately gives up seven runs. I'm embarrassed. The Pirates lose badly.

- 13 -

J.D.'S FAMILY is in Pittsburgh where they have a Memorial Day shindig every year. They all go to the Pirates doubleheader on Friday. Rob Mackowiak hits a walk-off grand slam in Game 1 and a ninth-inning game-tying home run in Game 2. J.D.'s mother and sister are forced to sit through 19 innings of exciting baseball. Later that night, Mackowiak's son is born.

Brennan and I make plans to go to the Saturday game. We pick J.D. up from his grandma's and head to the ballpark. We don't realize Pirates games ever sell out, but it's a fireworks night and we're stuck with standing-room-only tickets. We linger deep in left field before scouting out three abandoned seats up for grabs. With his hospital bracelet still on, Mackowiak hits another home run and drives in five runs total. Bucs win 10-7!

The next morning, Brennan and I can't reach J.D. to see if he can come to the Sunday game with us. We try calling for hours. Finally J.D. calls back just as Brennan and I are about to park twenty minutes before first pitch. I tell him I'm not going to pick him up this late and miss the beginning of the game. Brennan and I go to the game, get decent seats, and the Pirates get killed 12-1, punishing me for being a jerk.

Back in Rochester, J.D. wants to go to the bar to watch the Pirates. I'm supposed to do something with my girlfriend but I'd rather watch the game so I tell her I'll be over later than planned. J.D. and I have a great time and the Pirates actually win. Later, my girlfriend is mad that I blew her off. She makes me watch *Dirty Dancing* to make up for it. A win is a win, but at what cost?

- 14 -

I'M EXCITED about Zach Duke! I'm in attendance when he beats the Mets to begin his career 5-0. The New York newspapers crown him The Duke of New York. He's a rookie phenom no national outlet can ignore. I cut out every article on Duke I can find. His sophomore season isn't very good. In fact, he's never good again until he resurrects his career as a left-handed specialist in another team's bullpen. I throw out my Duke collection.

I'm driving back from Ontario with my soon-to-be fiancé (I'm proposing next week) and once we cross the border I call Dad for a Pirates update. The Pirates and Astros—probably the least interesting matchup in the Majors—are in extra innings. Dad calls me every inning to keep me up-to-date as the game goes into the eighteenth. After each call I relay the news to my girl-friend. She acts interested for my benefit. I drop her off and arrive home at nearly one in the morning. Dad is still up listening to the Pirates broadcast through the internet.

"Joshua! Come quick! Jason Bay is on third with no outs!" Fly ball…is it deep enough?…Bay tags…He's safe!…Pirates win! *There was nooooo doubt about it!*

Then I am a groomsman in Joe's wedding. Joe, a Yankees and Bills fan, pities me for liking the Pirates and envies me for liking the Steelers. Joe gives me groomsman gifts, a framed autographed picture of the 2006 Pirates and a Zach Duke autographed base-ball. Joe doesn't realize it, but the 18-inning victory did not spark an epic winning streak for the Pirates. Instead, we're nearing the end of arguably the most depressing season yet, what with the sharp drop-off from Duke's magical rookie campaign, bad free agent signings, trades for over-the-hill players, and the hir-ing of a guy who has become the least liked Pirates manager of all time.

Dad and I take a road trip and see the Pirates lose twice in St. Louis. The Cardinals fans are annoyingly polite; one fan nearby gushes about Jason Bay and hopes the Cardinals will sign him when he's a free agent. The next day, in Cincinnati, we see the Pirates score eight runs in the top of the tenth inning to beat the Reds. How refreshing to see another fan base so disgruntled.

Joe and I go to a short-season Single-A Batavia Muckdogs game. Our tickets say it's "Mormon Night", explaining why most of the men are wearing white shirts and black ties. 1960 NL Cy Young Award Winner Vern Law, The Deacon, is the guest of honor. Law pitched for Batavia back in the fifties when Batavia was affiliated with the Pirates. Law signs a baseball for me, and it replaces my Zach Duke ball.

- 15 -

WHEN THE PRESENT SUCKS this much, one clings to the past. I read dozens of baseball books in a row. David Maraniss humanizes Roberto Clemente brilliantly in his biography. *Moneyball* is read during this streak, as is Scott Pitoniak's *Baseball in Rochester*, and autobiographies by Willie Stargell and Steve Blass (of the Steve Blass Disease). *The Greatest Game Ever Played* is a pitch-for-pitch recount of Game 7 of the 1960 World Series—fascinating.

My wife buys me a 1911 Tobacco baseball card for my birthday. She looked specifically for a Pirate, and since Honus Wagner wasn't in her price range, she went with Lefty Leifield. I don't know much about Leifield. He gets mentioned briefly in Al Stump's formerly definitive biography of Ty Cobb; Cobb faced Leifield in the 1909 World Series. I make a note of it on the inside cover—page 178 if anyone's interested.

Of all the *auto*biographies I read, Bob Gibson's is my favorite, and not only because he describes Willie Stargell as the only opposing player he couldn't bring himself to hate. I grow to love Gibson as both a competitor and as a person. I root hard for the 1960s Cardinals. Gibson turns me into a huge Curt Flood fan, so much so that I seek Flood's out-of-print autobiography next. After reading it, though, I don't like Flood so much anymore. That's the way it works with autobiographies. I sympathize with Ted Williams and I adore Buck O'Neill, but Joe Morgan annoys me, and while I didn't like Reggie Jackson before, he's not so bad now.

- 16 -

MY BASEBALL FANDOM is in a vulnerable place during this period of reading. A lifetime of losing, basically, is draining. The Pirates have a new general manager with yet another plan to pull the team out of the dregs. He trades Jason Bay and Xavier Nady for eight prospects, none of whom pan out. Then my favorite player, Jack Wilson, is traded, as is Nate McLouth, just months after the GM singled him out as one of the cornerstones of the team. I'm depressed.

How much better life would be if I rooted for a different team. I've never seriously thought about it before.

- 17 -

CRITERIA FOR CHOOSING a new favorite team:

1.   Must play in American League
2.   No West Coast or Mountain Teams
3.   No large-market teams, i.e., Chicago, L.A., New York, Boston.
4.   Must have strong history, preferably one of the original 16 franchises.

CONTENDERS:

1.   St. Louis Cardinals. Based almost entirely on the Gibson autobiography, the Cardinals are the first obvious candidate for my new team. They have great history, as I've been reading, and I find myself trying to bring up Gibson and the 1964 and 1967 World Series in every baseball conversation I have. This really annoys J.D., who violently hates the Cardinals. I don't harbor much animosity for them, though. True, they beat up on the Pirates, but so does everyone else. However—and this is where criterion #1 comes in—even if I go off the Pirates cold turkey, I can't imagine myself rooting against them, and the Cardinals and Pirates play each other a lot. NL Central

teams are out. In fact, I cross off the entire National League.

2.   Tampa Bay Rays. The Rays are a serious contender because I'm currently going to school only a few hours away in Tallahassee. Tampa Bay took the "devil" out of their name and promptly put together their first franchise winning season and a trip to the World Series. Too, they play the Red Sox and Yankees a lot, and I hate them both. But the Rays have no history. Hanging above my desk are framed pictures of Roberto Clemente, Bill Mazeroski, and Willie Stargell. Which historically great Rays could replace them?

3.   Cleveland Indians. *Dad and I score tickets to Game 2 of the 2007 ALDS, Yankees at Cleveland. We both sport Pirates hats and get funny looks as we walk in. But we are fueled by a) our desire for relevant baseball and b) our hatred of the Yankees. We cheer with every pitch and slap fives with surrounding Indians fans who have accepted us as their own. In the eighth inning midges swarm the field, distracting the players, especially Joba Chamberlain on the mound, who gives up the tying run. 1-1. We cheer and yell, then hold our breaths as the pitch is delivered. Tonight we are HUGE Indians fans. Travis Hafner drives home the winning run in the eleventh. Tribe wins!* The cities of Pittsburgh and Cleveland sort of have a rivalry, but I've never actually lived in Pittsburgh so it's not much of

a deterrent. However, despite a bloodline that goes back over a hundred years, Indians history kind of blows, and the city in general has adopted an annoying "woe-is-me" attitude when it comes to sports.

4. Also rans:

A. Minnesota Twins. Pros: they go back awhile, especially if you include their years as the Washington Senators; Kirby Puckett's team; Rochester is now their Triple-A affiliate. But I'm an easterner and Minnesota is too far away; I'll never get there for a game.

B. Kansas City Royals. An expansion team in 1969 but the city's impressive Negro League history makes up for it. Currently, though, they're as hapless as the Pirates, and, like Minnesota, a little too far away.

C. Detroit Tigers. Pros: Detroit and Pittsburgh are similar cities; the Tigers were a flagship franchise with great history; baseball's ultimate bad guy Ty Cobb played here (Hemingway on Cobb: "the greatest of all ballplayers, and an absolute shit"). This seems like a solid choice, especially because most of their coaching staff are former Pirates managers. But they perennially underachieve despite their spend-happy offseasons, and in general the team rubs me the wrong way.

- 18 -

TWENTY-NINE other teams, but I'm sticking with the Pirates. There's always a reason to be optimistic. I've been reading about our top prospect for years, and Andrew McCutchen finally gets called up. I got his autograph a year ago when the Indianapolis Indians and I were both in Rochester and he strolled over to the stands where I called his name.

Dad flies down to Tallahassee and we leave from there on another road trip. We see a game in Tampa's awful indoor stadium. We see three Marlins games, each delayed by rain. Then we drive north to Atlanta where the Pirates are in town. This is McCutchen's fourth game as a Major Leaguer. My wife has been in Illinois for a conference the last few days but she meets us in Atlanta and comes to the game with us. Cutch has four hits including two triples, but the Pirates lose in fifteen innings. My wife is a good sport and sticks around until the bitter end.

- 19 -

"I'VE BEEN WAITING 115 years to get to the World Series."

"No you haven't, you idiot; you've been waiting your entire life, same as me!"

For decades Red Sox fans blamed the Curse of the Bambino. Cubs fans still blame the Billy Goat. But pick a point during the Pirates two-decade drought and ask "What exactly is the problem here?" and, instead of blaming some supernatural hocus pocus, most Pirates fans would respond, "the ownership is cheap, the management doesn't know what it's doing, and the players aren't very good."

So then why is it so hard to leave them behind?! My tie to Pennsylvania isn't *that* strong. Why is checking the Pirates score the first thing I think of when I wake up in the morning? I mean, even on Sundays when the Steelers take on the Seahawks, Cardinals, or Packers in the Super Bowl I still check the baseball news first.

Seinfeld has a bit about how we don't root for the players, we root for their shirts. A former player comes to town? "Boo! Different shirt! Boo!" It works the other way, too. A.J. Burnett was a Marlin but he quit on the team a few weeks before free agency, so I booed him. He signed with the Blue Jays but, after a few years, opted out of his contract (reason to boo) and signed with the Yankees (double reason to boo!). He wasn't very good for the Yankees, which was excellent. But now he wears a Pirates shirt and he's one of my favorite players.

My love for the Pirates wins out every time. I never made a choice; something was ingrained in me before I was able to make memories. It's heredity, like the color of one's eyes. It's involuntary, like breathing.

- 20 -

I'VE FATHERED A NEW Pirates fan. "Those are the Brewers," my boy says, pointing at the opponent on TV. "They're the bad guys." "That's right, bud. And that's Ryan Braun. He's the worst of the bad guys." My boy's lower lip starts to quiver. "Then why isn't he in jail?"

It doesn't seem that long ago that we completed his potty-training. No longer having to change poopy diapers represents a dramatic improvement in the quality of my life. Still, even that takes a backseat to the Pirates snapping their twenty-year losing streak.

A winning season, finally. They even make the playoffs! No one was sure this would ever happen. My wife—"I'm happy for you," she says; "Happy for us!" I insist—and I are watching the Pirates on a national stage. The fans lucky enough to go to the game don't take it for granted. They are raucous and passionate, and dressed in black, for intimidation, after several Pirates players called for a "blackout" on Twitter. The fans taunt Reds starting pitcher Johnny Cueto so loudly and relentlessly that he loses the grip on the ball and drops it on the ground! Cheers and jeers ensue. Next pitch, home run! Pirates win! I'm teary-eyed.

On Instant Messenger away messages, and later on Facebook, J.D. and I used to post things like

"Why are the Pittsburgh Pirates the worst team in the world?"

Life is better now.

[2013]

*E*ND

Joshua Britton is a professional trombonist living in Louisville, Kentucky with his wife and two children. He is the author of a short story collection, *Tadpoles*, and a novelette, *Heart Decisions,* and he served as editor for *The Notes Will Carry Me Home*.

www.joshua-britton.com

joshua_britton@yahoo.com

Twitter: @JP_Britton